"That Mouth [...] Going to Get [...] Serious Trouble ..."

"Tell me about it," she dared him.

"So you want to know something about me, do you?" Drew punctuated the question with a swift, hard kiss to her lips. "I am thirty-seven years old and definitely not married." He repeated the action a second time with even greater insistence. "Until a year ago I was president of Bradford Electronics. Corporate offices located in Albany, New York. I resigned that position but retain a seat on the board of directors." His third kiss was lingering, less harsh, less motivated by retribution than the others. "I've been teaching business courses here at Oneonta for the past twelve months and up until a few days ago led a very comfortable existence."

Then he came to her a fourth time, lingering over her mouth, relishing its warmth and sweetness. This kiss was thorough. It was everything a kiss should be—driving, demanding, bittersweet to the point of tears. . . .

SUZANNE SIMMS

was born in Storm Lake, Iowa, and currently lives in Indiana with her husband and nine-year-old son. She has a degree in English literature, loves opera, and studied classical piano for ten years. She loves reading and writing romances and believes being a successful romance writer is primary a matter of attitude.

Dear Reader;

SILHOUETTE DESIRE is an exciting new line of contemporary romances from Silhouette Books. During the past year, many Silhouette readers have written in telling us what other types of stories they'd like to read from Silhouette, and we've kept these comments and suggestions in mind in developing SILHOUETTE DESIRE.

DESIREs feature all of the elements you like to see in a romance, plus a more sensual, provocative story. So if you want to experience all the excitement, passion and joy of falling in love, then SILHOUETTE DESIRE is for you.

I hope you enjoy this book and all the wonderful stories to come from SILHOUETTE DESIRE. I'd appreciate any thoughts you'd like to share with us on new SILHOUETTE DESIRE, and I invite you to write to us at the address below:

Jane Nicholls
Silhouette Books
PO Box 177
Dunton Green
Sevenoaks
Kent
TN13 2YE

SUZANNE SIMMS
Of Passion Born

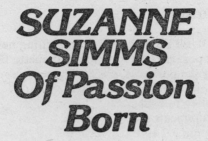

Silhouette Desire

Published by Silhouette Books

Copyright © 1982 by Suzanne Guntrum

First printing 1983

British Library C.I.P.

Simms, Suzanne
  Of passion born.—(Silhouette desire)
  I. Title
  813'.54[F]   PS3569.I/

  ISBN 0 340 32928 9

Printed and bound in Great Britain for
Hodder and Stoughton Paperbacks, a
division of Hodder and Stoughton Ltd.,
Mill Road, Dunton Green, Sevenoaks,
Kent (Editorial Office: 47 Bedford
Square, London, WC1 3DP) by
Richard Clay (The Chaucer Press) Ltd.,
Bungay, Suffolk

Of Passion Born

1

~~~~~~~~~~

The young woman astride the Schwinn "Traveler" paused at the stone bridge that marked the front entrance to the park. Leaning the handlebars of her bicycle against a thick buttress, she peered down into the clear water of the creek, calling to mind innumerable other times she must have paused at this very spot as a girl. In the spring Wilber Creek, swollen by heavy rains and melted snow, was a rushing, churning force. But now at summer's end, it lazily meandered along its sinuous course.

While there was a discernible briskness to the early morning air, there was no real indication on this day in late August that fall was on its way. Still Chelsie McBride knew from experience that in the weeks ahead October maples ablaze with scarlet and gold would transform the lush green park with their colorful autumnal cloak.

Chelsie was very glad she had made the decision to return to this central New York State college town for the fall semester. Autumn had always been her favorite season of the year, especially here in Oneonta, as the "City of the Hills" was aptly named.

A small community on the Susquehanna River, Oneonta was nestled where three valleys came together, its rolling hills and mountains typical of the western slope of the Catskills. A century and a half ago, the valley had been practically a virgin wilderness, with only a few scattered pioneer settlements. Now it was a thriving community with numerous businesses and two colleges to its credit.

But less factual matters were on her mind as Chelsie pushed off the abutment, her long, well-shaped legs moving in a fluid motion as she pedaled down the park road. She leaned slightly forward in anticipation of the approaching hill that would lead her further into Wilber Park.

A nostalgic half-smile pulled at the corners of her generous mouth as she spotted at one side of the road the well-worn path she had strolled along as a girl, often with umbrella in hand, acting out the roles of her favorite fictional characters, from Sherlock Holmes to the Count of Monte Cristo. She had been something of a dreamer then, frequently living in a make-believe world of magic and mysticism, chivalry and unrequited love.

Chelsie McBride held only affection in her heart for that girl now. At twenty-eight she had long since left the world of make-believe behind. Still, there was an unexpected sense of relief that this place of childhood memories had not changed so very much in the intervening years.

Then of necessity she concentrated her energies on getting up the steep slope in front of her. Tiny drops of perspiration formed on her upper lip and forehead as she pedaled harder. On reaching the summit a sense of well-being washed over her. It felt good to push her body to its physical as well as its mental limits. Chelsie was suddenly very glad she had gone to the trouble of bringing her bicycle with her.

At the crest of the hill she paused for a moment to savor the still quiet of the morning. The park seemed undisturbed by human occupation at this early hour. She shoved off again, the cooling breeze welcome on her overheated skin. She presented an attractive picture in a warm-up suit of deep blue terrycloth that accented her blue eyes. The sun filtering down through the trees caught the golden highlights that naturally streaked her hair in the summertime. Her cheeks were slightly flushed from the exertion, adding a healthy sheen to her complexion. The casual clothing she wore did little to camouflage the curves beneath that were just on the slim side of voluptuous.

Lightly pressing her sneakered feet to the pedals, she changed gears as the bicycle sped down the other side of the hill. She threw her head back in carefree abandon and gazed up at the checkered pattern of light and dark created by the giant elms that spanned the roadway like a canopy. Then without warning she had reached the bottom of the hill and was racing round a sharp curve.

Chelsie was trying to slow her progress when seemingly out of nowhere a man appeared on foot. She had only a fraction of a second to register his presence and the traditional gray sweat suit he was

wearing before she slammed on the brakes. The
ten-speed bicycle skidded along the berm of the road,
colliding with the solid male body before crashing to a
halt in the prickly underbrush.

"Oh—damn!" came the groaned expletive, as the
cyclist untangled her arms and legs from the wreck-
age. She began to brush herself off, checking for
damage to the Schwinn as well as to her person, when
she realized the man was still lying at the edge of the
road, his eyes closed. Chelsie rushed to his side,
dropping to her knees in the gravel.

Her initial reaction was a barely audible "Dear
God!" With shaky tentative movements, her hands
explored the man's arms and chest and torso, searching for broken bones or worse.

A terrible wheezing sound emanated from the inert
form of the man as he came to life. He drew in short
and obviously painful breaths of air. At last his eyes
flickered open and Chelsie found herself staring down
into gray-green depths that actually sent a shudder
through her body.

"I-I want to h-help. . . ." she stammered rather
badly, a feeling of helplessness overriding her usual
coolheaded efficiency.

That the man was unable to answer her became
clear in a matter of seconds. Chelsie unconsciously
grasped his hand in hers and waited for him to regain
his breath.

"Knocked the wind out of me. . . ." The man finally
explained in a form of verbal shorthand.

"Please—let me help you," insisted Chelsie, as the
stranger attempted to sit up. Somehow in the process
his head came up at the same instant hers went down
and they literally collided head-on!

"Damn!" growled her victim, as he fell back into the gravel, his eyes clouding anew with pain.

"I'm sorry," Chelsie mumbled, as she blinked back the spontaneous tears that rushed to her own eyes. She carefully rubbed the point of impact just below her hairline.

After some time, the man again tried to struggle into a sitting position.

"Please—" Chelsie started to reiterate her offer.

"No!" That one word cut the air like a knife. "I would prefer you didn't try to help." He gave her a quick, penetrating look, his voice deep and his words slowly spaced. "You are a dangerous young woman," the man observed censoriously. "Why don't you stay the hell off the road until you learn how to ride that thing?"

A flush of embarrassed color rose on her cheeks. "I said I was sorry," she repeated as calmly as she could. "I scarcely make a habit of running down pedestrians," she offered in her own defense.

Trying not to groan, the man got to his feet. "You know," he said through gritted teeth, "you're just damned lucky I wasn't a Volkswagen bus. What the hell possessed you to come barreling around that curve without even looking where you were going?" The condescending tone with which he asked the question indicated all too clearly his opinion of her intelligence—or lack of it.

"It was purely an accident. I. . . ." Chelsie started to explain, then changed her mind. "I said I was sorry for running into you. Are you sure you aren't hurt?"

"Oh, I'm fine—other than a broken rib or two," he said with grim humor, gingerly rubbing a hand along the wall of his chest.

Chelsie was tempted to pluck the tangle of dead leaves and twigs from his sleeve, but something in the stranger's manner prevented her from doing so. She found herself imagining the feel of the hard, steely muscles beneath the sweat shirt, as she stood staring at him. She took in for the first time the dark brown hair that was scattered with gray and a few dead leaves that she had helped put there, the cool gray eyes that stated quite expressively his opinion of irresponsible cyclists, the well-developed chest and shoulders that made her wonder if he were a boxer of some sort.

The man did not measure so very much more than her own five and a half feet; he was the taller by no more than four or five inches. It was his physique, she decided, that made him seem to be a bigger man than he really was. But the face was what captured Chelsie's attention and forced her to reassess her hazarded guess at his occupation.

It was a strong face, an intelligent face, with rather thick arched brows, a straight, well-defined nose, and a firmly set mouth. Not particularly attractive when broken down into its components, it was devastating as a whole. There was a certain aura of command about the man as well, an attitude of latent power, even as they stood there quietly assessing each other and the damage wrought by her carelessness.

Then Chelsie McBride suddenly recognized what was really different about him. Showing none of the usual reactions she had come to expect—to put up with—from most of the male populace, this man was regarding her as if he simply did not see her. He appeared totally blind to the length of silky hair, the startling blue eyes that darkened to midnight when she was angry, the shapely form that usually drew at least a once-over. In point of fact, *this* man seemed only interested in getting away from her.

How odd, thought Chelsie, to be aware of this stranger's physical attributes while he apparently remained immune to hers. The shoe had indeed been put on the other foot and it was a new experience for her. And how like her to try to put it in genteel terms when in plain simple English this man was sexy as hell!

Chelsie told herself to take a second look at the situation and examine it quite without emotion. It was possible—she supposed—that he was farsighted and had simply forgotten to wear his glasses. Or perhaps he had seen too many beautiful women in his years— years that must be somewhere between thirty-five and forty—and therefore, her attractions paled by comparison. Or maybe he wasn't interested in *women*—God forbid! Or perhaps the man did not find *her* attractive. Once she got started, Chelsie saw that the list could go on and on.

Her eyes traveled reluctantly back to his as she realized he was speaking. "I beg your pardon. . . ."

The skin of the man's face seemed to tighten. "I said—watch where you're going in the future, young lady, or your next victim may not be so lucky—nor may you!"

Really, he had no sense of humor, Chelsie thought. "Perhaps joggers should be required by law to wear warning bells on their shoes to let people know they're coming," she said, half in jest.

The man gave her one of those looks that did indeed replace a thousand well-chosen words.

Chelsie immediately regretted giving in to the urge to say something so obviously silly, especially to this man. It was one thing to respond with one of her famous barbs to a cheeky student or an overamorous faculty member, but this was a complete stranger she had mown down with her Schwinn, and surely he deserved better treatment at her hands.

"I'm sorry," she finally managed to stammer, "that was a rather idiotic thing to say."

"I usually don't believe in apologies. They aren't worth the breath it takes to say them." The man looked at her until Chelsie uncomfortably let her eyes drop before his. "But in your case I've decided to make an exception. Apology accepted—on the second count only, of course, not for using your bicycle like a bulldozer." When she glanced up there was a small, self-satisfied smile on his lips.

Her mouth started to work furiously, but no sound came out. She was still trying to think of an appropriate comeback when the man brushed past her and took off at a run in the direction he had originally been headed. Without so much as a backward glance he disappeared around the curve in the road.

"Well—I never!" exclaimed Chelsie McBride. She was still mumbling and grumbling as she retrieved her bicycle from the brush. It was with far greater care, if less joy, that she resumed her ride through the park.

A half hour later Chelsie pedaled up the driveway of the big old rambling house on Irving Place where she had rented an apartment for the fall. Esther Freeman, the owner and landlady, was out pruning dead blooms from a flower bed at the side of the building.

The Freeman house was typical of those built in Oneonta after the turn of the century. Of no particular architectural style, it had once been a majestic three-story family home. In recent years it had of necessity been divided into apartments to keep its owner from forfeiting her home and entering an apartment herself.

Mrs. Freeman retained the first floor for her own use. Chelsie had rented half of the second story, and another woman occupied the remainder. The third-floor garret housed Mrs. Freeman's nephew, a rather innocuous young man, at least according to Esther Freeman, who taught American history at the local high school.

"Good morning, Dr. McBride!" hailed the woman, as she straightened up from her task, a handful of wilted blooms in her apron. "How was your bicycle ride?"

"Fine . . . thank you," Chelsie responded, deliberately avoiding any mention of her encounter with the jogger.

"Are you settling in all right? Be sure to let me know if there's anything you need. I do want you to feel this is your home for as long as you stay with us," Esther Freeman went on, rather loquacious for the early hour.

"That's very kind of you," Chelsie said with sincerity. She had taken an immediate liking to her landlady upon her arrival yesterday, but prolonged conversation was beyond her until she'd had at least one cup of coffee. "I'd better get my bike put away. I have lots of unpacking to do before the faculty meeting this afternoon."

"Have a grand day, dearie!" The woman cheerfully called after Chelsie. Then she once more bent to her task.

Chelsie stowed her Schwinn at the side of the wide verandalike porch that extended along the front and down both sides of the house. There was a private stairway to her apartment that she preferred to use rather than the commonly held front entrance.

When she had agreed to Dr. Nelson's request to teach a semester at the State University College at Oneonta, discreet inquiries had been made for her to find a set of furnished rooms that wouldn't cost the sun and the moon. Her studio apartment at Bryn Mawr had been sublet to a visiting professor from the University of North Wales, but even so, Dr. Chelsie McBride found she had to budget carefully.

No one got rich teaching. Chelsie had even resorted to her once considerable skills as a seamstress over the summer and had fashioned herself a good-looking wardrobe of mix-and-match skirts, vests, and blazers, in current styles and colors. The designer labels that could skyrocket a price tag into the hundreds of dollars for one outfit were out of reach of her pocketbook.

She climbed the flight of steps and unlocked the door to her apartment. It was quite honestly a disaster area. She had driven up from Pennsylvania the day before, unpacking only the essentials last night before falling into bed. She definitely needed a hot shower and a cup of coffee before she could face the pile of odd boxes and suitcases in the middle of what was supposed to be her living room.

Mrs. Freeman's was just the kind of place Chelsie loved. Big, high-ceilinged rooms with touches reminiscent of an age when craftsmanship was still appreciated and encouraged. Of course, there had been extensive remodeling done, but as she surveyed the comfortably furnished apartment she knew how lucky she was to have it. Yes, these three rooms would do her very nicely for the semester.

Throwing off the warm-up suit, Chelsie went into the bathroom for a quick shower while the drip coffeemaker gurgled on the kitchen counter. Fifteen minutes later she emerged dressed in jeans and a smock, her hair still damp. She flipped the dial from "brew" to "warm" and helped herself to one of the mugs hanging in a neat row from the cabinet. Then she settled in a big overstuffed chaise and absently studied the scene in front of her as she sipped her coffee.

There was a portable stereo and a selection of records from Vivaldi to Juice Newton, a foldaway bookcase that just as quickly and easily unfolded, two corrugated boxes of notes and reference books for the classes she would be teaching, another box of odds and ends, a set of luggage filled with clothes, and a steamer trunk that contained winter coats, boots, and the like. And there were still a few miscellaneous items in her AMC Eagle parked in the driveway below. Howard Freeman had been indispensable in helping her move the entire cache from car to apartment, she had to admit. And if she wanted to return the rented U-haul before the two o'clock faculty meeting, she would have to get to work.

Chelsie unfolded her legs and buckled down to making a serious attempt at organization. The apartment itself was spotless, thanks to Esther Freeman. She set up the folding walnut bookcase next to the desk and spent the next hour unpacking and filing her books and papers. With that job completed to her satisfaction, Chelsie hauled the suitcases into the bedroom and went to work putting her clothes in some semblance of order.

She had just stowed the luggage and several of the

now empty boxes in the large hall closet, when a knock came at the door to her apartment. With an unconscious pat to the natural wave of her hair, she swung open the door.

"Hello!" Standing in the hallway was a pleasant-looking young woman, attractively attired in a red cotton sundress that showed her olive skin and dark brown hair to advantage. "I know you're getting settled in this morning, but I wanted to stop by and introduce myself. I'm Lynn Marshall, your neighbor."

"Hi, Lynn. I'm Chelsie McBride." The smile was returned with a handshake.

"Yes, I know. Mrs. Freeman told me your name," the woman hastened to explain. "You're teaching at the State University this fall, aren't you? I'm freshman French myself."

"English Lit," grinned Chelsie, pointing to herself. "I was just about to take a well-deserved coffee break. Would you like to join me?"

"I'd love to if you're sure I'm not interrupting your unpacking," responded Lynn, stepping inside at the invitation.

"Not at all, but you'll have to overlook the mess," warned Chelsie. "I tried to bring only the necessities with me, but apparently the necessities ran to quite a lot in my case," she laughed.

"I've been renting from Esther Freeman for nearly two years now and you appear to be more organized in one day than I am after all that time," Lynn Marshall confessed rather sheepishly.

"How do you take your coffee?" Chelsie asked her guest, as she took another mug from the kitchen cupboard and poured them each a cup.

"Cream and sugar—but only if you have it," answered the brunette.

"They were the first things I unpacked after the coffeemaker and coffee. I've never been able to drink mine black." Chelsie found herself chatting to Lynn Marshall as if they were somehow old friends. "I'm afraid all I have to offer with the coffee is half a box of stale vanilla wafers. I haven't had a chance to get to the grocery store yet."

"Stale vanilla wafers are one of my favorites," smiled the other woman, the hint of a dimple appearing in each cheek. "Thanks, but just coffee will be fine."

"You mentioned you've been living at Mrs. Freeman's for two years now. Is that how long you've been teaching at Oneonta?" Chelsie inquired once they had settled down in the only two chairs her living room sported.

This drew a nod from Lynn Marshall. "After I finished my master's degree I taught a year in a junior college upstate, but I've always loved this area. When an opening came up in first year French, I immediately put in my application. I'm a hometown girl—I don't know if that was a point in my favor or not. Anyway, I got the position, and *voilà*, I've been here ever since," she ended rather modestly. Chelsie was certain the woman's credentials were far more impressive than she had intimated. "How about you?" Lynn asked interestedly.

"I've been at Bryn Mawr the past couple of years. Then Dr. Nelson approached me early last spring about taking a special sabbatical and coming to Oneonta for the fall semester." Chelsie set her coffee on the side table and curled her legs underneath her. She tucked her hair behind her ears in a habitual gesture. "I thought the change would be good for me and I think I've always wanted to come back here somehow. This gave me the perfect opportunity," she concluded.

Lynn Marshall had been unabashedly studying her as she spoke. Finally, the brunette blurted out what was on her mind. "I know this sounds trite, but there is something about you that seems so familiar. McBride . . . McBride. . . ." The woman tapped a perfectly buffed nail against her lower lip.

"Lynn Marshall? You—you wouldn't be Gerry Marshall's sister?" Chelsie ventured to guess, not really knowing.

"The very one!" Lynn beamed, her face lighting up as if she had just solved the mystery of the ages. "And you are Chelsie McBride—vice-president of the junior class, honor society, Girls' Leader Club, and Thespians! You were my idol when we were in high school. My God, it's a small world." Lynn Marshall looked positively floored.

"I don't believe this," murmured Chelsie. In the next breath she promptly contradicted herself. "I don't know why it took me so long to put two and two together. I should have guessed the minute you said you were a hometown girl."

"Let's face it, it has been a few years," chuckled Lynn. "I was a year behind you and Gerry. I should have recognized you. But you didn't graduate from Oneonta High, did you?"

"No, I didn't. My family moved to Pennsylvania after my junior year," Chelsie said rather wistfully. It had been the only one of numerous moves her family had made that had caused regret on her part.

"Well, Gerry will certainly be surprised to hear you're back in town. I remember you two had a thing going there for awhile. Of course, my brother was something of a pain in those days," Lynn acknowledged with a grin.

Yes—at least *she* had had a thing for Gerry Marshall the last spring she had lived in Oneonta, thought Chelsie. She had imagined herself to be in love with Gerry. And, yes, he had been something of a pain. But that had been so many years ago now. She had learned to put the past where it belonged—in the past.

"How is Gerry?" she finally asked, more out of politeness than any great curiosity.

"Better now, but he was making a real mess of it there for awhile. He dropped out of college after his sophomore year and married Becky Thurman. They had two kids before they decided they couldn't make a go of it. Gerry has got his act together at last. He's working at the newspaper during the day and taking classes at night to finish his degree. Quite honestly, after seeing the hell my brother put himself through I've been pretty cautious about getting married myself," Lynn said with candor.

"I know exactly what you mean," Chelsie stated with feeling, picking up the thread of the conversation. "I've seen so many of my friends and acquaintances suffer through divorce. I want no part of it—thanks, anyway!"

She had also seen the sometimes sad, sometimes frantic world of her single friends, and Chelsie McBride had not cared for what she saw there, either.

To her, marriage was the undying devotion her parents had shared for forty years. If she couldn't have that kind of marriage she preferred to have none. Truth be known, Chelsie was a bit of a romantic underneath all the layers of acquired sophistication. Her mind sought a man her equal. Her heart wished for moonlight and roses.

Evidently Lynn Marshall felt the need to move on to another subject and she did so gracefully. "Tell me— what have you seen since you got back?" she asked with genuine interest.

"Not much, I'm afraid," Chelsie responded with a lighthearted laugh. "When I got into town last night I went by the house we lived in on East Street and took a quick drive around the campus. It's really changed since I was last here. With the Lab school closed, Old Main torn down, the upper level of the campus expanded. . . ." She shook her head. "I'm going to need a map just to get around. Oh—and I took a bicycle ride through Wilber Park earlier this morning." She made an airy little gesture with her fingers. "I nearly wiped out one of the local residents, too."

"And you've only been back in town less than twenty-four hours," teased her companion. "So tell me, what happened?" Lynn prompted, leaning forward in her chair.

"Well, I was riding along minding my own business when I took the curve at the bottom of the big hill a little too fast and ran smack dab into this man," she said. "Laid him out flat, too."

"You didn't!" Lynn exclaimed, lifting one eyebrow. There was something about certain people—people like Chelsie McBride—that made even the ordinary events of their lives interesting. "What was he like?" she asked, curious in spite of herself.

"I don't know." Chelsie shrugged as though she hadn't paid that much attention to the man. "He was rather good-looking in an athletic sort of way, I suppose. You know—the jock type."

Lynn Marshall concealed a smile. "Young?"

"Hm . . . he was probably thirty-five, anyway," murmured Chelsie thoughtfully. "Dark hair with some gray. Unusual eyes, kind of gray and green. They seemed to change color with his mood."

"Yes—and I can imagine what his mood was at being run down," the brunette commented with a wry smile.

"I'm not sure which stunned him more—the impact of my bike or the idea that he wasn't as invincible as he'd thought." As she made the observation, Chelsie suddenly knew somehow that it was true. It hadn't occurred to her earlier, but by God, she'd hit upon something—something besides the man in the park, that was.

"You no doubt bruised the man's ego," suggested Lynn.

"Apparently—along with a rib or two. He was pretty decent about it, although he did insinuate I was a rather unintelligent creature, as I recall. I believe his exact words were 'why don't you stay the hell off the road until you learn how to ride that thing?' "

"You didn't tell him who you are?"

"We never actually got around to exchanging names," said Chelsie with a shaky laugh. "He seemed most eager to be on his way."

"I'll bet he was." Lynn Marshall lost her air of

flippancy and took on one of practical concern. "I've enjoyed the conversation and the coffee, but it's time I let you get back to your unpacking. Thanks for the coffee," she said, carrying her mug to the kitchen.

Chelsie escorted her guest to the door. "It's been fun finding an old friend my first day back, Lynn. I'm glad you came by."

"If there is anything I can do to help, please let me know. I mean that sincerely." The woman turned back to Chelsie, chewing on her bottom lip for a moment, then spoke again. "If you're like me—and I think you are—you value your privacy. But if you should feel the need for company, I'm just across the hall out there."

Chelsie liked that. She was a little hesitant to make hasty friendships with anyone, male or female. "Thank you, Lynn. I'll probably see you at the faculty meeting this afternoon. I'm going up to the campus to locate my cubicle after I return the rented U-haul on my car."

"Cubicle is right. You've seen those wall plaques— 'Cubicle Sweet Cubicle'? Well, it definitely applies in our case. See you later, Chelsie—and don't run down any more gorgeous men in the meantime!" With a wave of her hand, Lynn Marshall disappeared around the corner and into her own apartment.

Odd, thought Chelsie, she couldn't remember telling Lynn the stranger in the park was gorgeous. Still, she was surprised to discover she could picture him quite clearly in her mind's eye. And there had been that peculiar feeling in the pit of her stomach as she had hovered above him, groping along his hard male body for injury.

She had chalked the feeling up to natural concern at

the time. But would she have had the same reaction if the man had been less attractive? If his voice had proven to be something less intriguing than that resonant baritone?

"Chelsie McBride, you were never one to be taken in by a pretty face and a set of muscles! Where are your standards, woman?" Only after she said them, did Chelsie realize the significance of her words.

The man was probably a blooming idiot, she told herself as she stepped back inside her apartment and firmly closed the door. Face it—there were so few men who had both an attractive exterior and an interesting mind that those who did tended to be insufferably conceited.

Well, she still had one more box she wanted to get unpacked, not to mention the sundry items in her Eagle. She'd better get a move on if she intended to have it all done before the faculty meeting.

Besides, she reminded herself as she hauled the box into the kitchen, after having been run over in that fashion by her bicycle, he was sure not to want to meet up with her again. Hadn't he accused her of being a dangerous young woman?

"Dangerous—my foot!" laughed Chelsie, as she went to work.

2

~~~~~~~~~~~~~~~~

Chelsie closed the door of her office, which had indeed turned out to be little more than the cubicle foretold by Lynn Marshall, and briskly walked down the corridor toward the faculty meeting room, her stiletto heels clicking on the tile floor with military precision. With each step she took the swath of thick golden-brown hair casually brushed against her shoulders.

The young professor was wearing a stylish dress with slightly padded shoulders, cinched waist, and a narrow skirt that ended just below the knee. It was not a creation of her own making, but a Samuel Blue label that had been within the modest means of her bank account. It was also one of her favorite dresses and for that reason alone she had chosen to wear it her first day on campus. The clinging mauve material patterned with tiny blue flowers complemented her fair coloring, which was more that of a blond than a brunette, and the cut of the dress was especially flattering to her figure.

Chelsie knew in a desultory kind of way that she was attractive, but with her too generous lower lip, a nose a bit too straight, and ears she felt should have been smaller and closer to her head, she would not have rated herself a beauty. She had forgotten that to be one of a kind, an original, was a form of beauty in itself.

As Chelsie slipped in the door of the large conference room, she beheld a vast sea of faces. Not that she minded—she had been the "new kid in class" too many times in her life for a roomful of strangers to prove intimidating now. She looked about her, vaguely recognizing a face or two in the throng.

She had advanced no more than a few feet into the room when a familiar figure wound its way toward her through the milling crowd.

"I think I would have known you anywhere," smiled the portly bespectacled gentleman, "even if Dr. Nelson hadn't told me of your return."

"Mr. Myers!" Chelsie exclaimed with unreserved pleasure, as she gave the man an awkward hug—awkward only because of the difference in their heights. She had been the taller of the two even back in the eighth grade when Arthur Myers had been her mathematics teacher.

"My . . . my . . ." the man said with a blush, "you're not the little Chelsie I sent to the lavatory to wash off that bright red lipstick, are you?"

"No, I'm not," she chuckled.

Then they laughed in unison at his reference to only one of many incidents that had occurred while she was his student. What this dear man had had to put up with, mused Chelsie. The growing pains of her youth had all passed before his knowing eyes.

"It's good to see you, Mr. Myers," she stated unequivocally.

"You're a beautiful woman now, *Doctor* Chelsie McBride. James and Claire must be very proud of you. How are your parents, by the way?"

"They're both well, thank you. Mother and Dad are living in Florida now," she replied.

"Yes, so I had heard. You know, we always regretted your father's decision to leave Oneonta. My, how the years have flown. To think that you have come back as a distinguished professor. . . ." Arthur Myers shook his head bemusedly.

"I don't know about the 'distinguished' part, but it is wonderful to be back," she assented.

"Hello, Professor Myers. I see you found your way after all, Chelsie." Lynn Marshall managed to greet both of them in a single breath.

"Yes, but I must confess I used a map," grinned Chelsie.

"Hello, Miss Marshall," acknowledged the man. "I take it you two know each other."

"We're neighbors—literally. Our apartments are directly across the hall from each other," volunteered his former pupil.

"And we attended Oneonta High School together," added Lynn.

"You said it yourself, Lynn. However much a cliché, it is a small world. Mr.—ah—Professor Myers was my eighth grade math teacher."

"And Dr. McBride was my star pupil," announced the man with a mischievous twinkle in his eye. "Well, welcome back to Oneonta, my dear. It was a pleasure, Miss Marshall." Arthur Myers exchanged a handshake with each woman. "It might be wise to find yourselves a seat now. The meeting should begin momentarily."

With his departure, Lynn and Chelsie weaved their way through the crowd toward two empty chairs at the back of the conference room. As she took her seat, Chelsie had the oddest sensation that someone's eyes were boring into her. It was not something she could recall ever happening before. In fact, she had always been rather skeptical of the old adage about "strangers across a crowded room." Nevertheless, she turned slightly in her chair and out of the corner of her eye caught a glimpse of a man standing on the opposite side of the hall.

Chelsie recognized him immediately. "Dear Lord!" she breathed through her teeth, her heart giving a leap.

"Are you all right?" Lynn inquired, upon seeing her friend go a bright crimson.

"Don't turn around! Please, not yet," Chelsie murmured, putting a restraining hand on Lynn Marshall's arm. "In a minute or so, would you turn to your left and see if you can tell me who the dark-haired man in the blue suede sport coat is?"

Lynn Marshall did it beautifully. Some moments later she managed to maneuver herself into position and nonchalantly glance over her companion's shoulder as requested. Then she made her report.

"That, my dear Chelsie, is none other than Professor Andrew Bradford—the heart throb of every female in Oneonta under the age of eighty and professor of business extraordinaire." The words came tumbling out of the side of her mouth.

"Professor Andrew Bradford. . . ." Chelsie repeated, testing the sound of his name.

By now Lynn was bursting with curiosity. "Why?" she demanded, feeling she deserved an answer as payment for her snooping.

"Because *that* is the man I ran over in the park this morning," Chelsie said with a sort of groan.

Lynn's jaw dropped in amazement. "You're kidding!"

"I only wish I were," Chelsie muttered in a low, earnest voice.

"I've heard he's some kind of physical fitness nut. I suppose that would explain why he was out jogging in the park." Lynn Marshall paused for emphasis. "Of all the people you could pick to run over. . . ."

Chelsie McBride gave a short, dry laugh. "I didn't exactly *pick* Andrew Bradford. It was simply one of those stupid accidents. Ah—there's Dr. Nelson now," she pointed out, settling back in her chair. "The meeting must be about to begin."

That effectively ended any discussion of Professor Andrew Bradford. Chelsie, for one, was very glad for the distraction. The realization that she had run down another member of the University faculty was proving to be a great embarrassment to her. In light of what she had just learned, she needed time to collect her wits.

Her attention was willingly focused on Daniel Nelson, president of the State University College at Oneonta, one of the seventy different institutions that make up the State University of New York. After welcoming the staff to the fall semester and proceeding with the usual kind of opening remarks, Dr. Nelson introduced the various deans, department heads, and other key members of the teaching staff. Much to her surprise and chagrin, Chelsie realized she was to be included in the latter.

"The final introduction is one I make with great personal pleasure," he began. "We have with us this semester, on special leave from Bryn Mawr College, a young but already well-respected Chaucerian scholar. A graduate of Bryn Mawr herself, with a doctorate from the University of Pennsylvania—Dr. Chelsie Mc-Bride."

With that brief resume of her credentials, Dr. Nelson requested that she stand for a moment. It was not a request that could be gracefully ignored, and while she would have preferred at least a word of warning, Chelsie rose to her feet nonetheless, a smile pasted on her face.

Daniel Nelson continued speaking as she stood. "For those of us who have been at Oneonta for some years, we say 'welcome back' to Chelsie. It is a pleasure and an honor to have another Dr. McBride gracing our staff."

"Thank you," she said pleasantly, but succinctly, as she resumed her place.

For a few minutes Chelsie had quite frankly forgotten Andrew Bradford's existence. At least until she regained her seat and in the process inadvertently caught his eye. Chelsie knew he was watching her, but the expression on his face—if a seemingly total lack of expression could be called that—was indecipherable.

Chelsie had thought herself a reasonably good judge of character, but this man was giving her second thoughts about that claim. One might have expected curiosity or surprise or even amusement, she told herself—even from him. None of these were evident. Apparently Andrew Bradford was one of those rare men who are able to conceal all or most of what they are thinking. That was her conclusion, anyway.

Then her attention once more reverted to the front of the room as the dean taking Dr. Nelson's place began a discussion of scheduling and other mundane matters necessitated by the start of any new semester. A half hour later the meeting was officially concluded and a general invitation was extended for coffee and refreshments, which were being set out on tables at one side of the conference room.

As they got to their feet, Lynn Marshall gave Chelsie a friendly poke. "Would a highly respected Chaucerian scholar care to join a rather ordinary French teacher for a cup of coffee?"

Chelsie had the good grace to go rather red in the face. "Oh, Lynn, I don't know why he did that. I had no idea Dr. Nelson was going to make such a fuss."

"A well-deserved fuss from what he said. And don't worry about Professor Andrew Bradford," Lynn quickly tacked on, seeing her companion's guarded surveillance of the crowd. "I see the indomitable Miss Crawford has him cornered. Even the best of them can't escape her clutches in under a half hour." The woman's dark eyes flickered with humor. "Rumor has it, Edith Crawford has been in these hallowed halls since the days when the college was officially known as the Oneonta State Normal School."

Chelsie McBride let out with a rollicking laugh. "In that case, more power to Miss Crawford! And I would love to have a cup of coffee with you, *s'il vous plaît.*"

Lynn Marshall's perfectly formed eyebrows rose a fraction of an inch. "Has anyone ever told you that your French accent is really quite. . . ."

". . . atrocious?"

"Well—" She drew out the double consonant. "I wouldn't have put it quite *that* way."

"Why not?" Chelsie reassured her in the same vein of good humor. "Half a dozen French teachers did along the way. Now come on before all those luscious-looking cookies are gone. I didn't have time for lunch. Hmmm . . . these sure beat stale vanilla wafers," mumbled Chelsie, as they each gobbled down several of the delectable pastries.

"There speaks a true gourmand," observed her cohort, as she indelicately licked her lips.

"Oh, Lynn—we're supposed to be dignified college professors and here you've got me giggling as if we were back in high school. I don't know when I've laughed so much." Chelsie wiped her cheeks with the back of her hand, using the diversion to surreptitiously check on a certain man's progress with the inimitable Miss Crawford. She spied Edith Crawford immediately, but Andrew Bradford was nowhere in sight. Apparently, he had the cunning to be the one who got away.

Somehow, not knowing where he was made Chelsie edgy. She had fully intended to keep one eye on him, and if absolutely necessary, make a quick getaway. Then she saw him halfway across the room, intently listening to a rather animated conversation. If he was working his way in her direction—and Chelsie wasn't at all sure that he was—then Professor Andrew Bradford might well prove to be a man to watch. The sly, cunning type—which type he could easily be—

were all the more to be avoided. Having found men to
be rather shallow and untrustworthy creatures, Chelsie told herself she should consider this one with a
healthy dose of skepticism.

She finally brought her gaze back to Lynn Marshall
with a wrenching effort, to be introduced by the
brunette to several of her friends on the faculty.
Chelsie groaned inwardly as her attention was once
more effectively diverted from Professor Bradford.

At the next opportunity that presented itself, Chelsie
sought out the now familiar breadth of blue suede
shoulder. She was rather disgusted with herself for
allowing a growing awareness of this man to dominate
her thoughts and actions at every turn. She seemed to
be conscious of Andrew Bradford all the while she
made inane and absent conversation with people she
hardly saw.

Then she realized she had a clear view of him over
Lynn Marshall's right shoulder. He couldn't be more
than ten or fifteen feet from their own little group.

Dear Lord, but he was a handsome devil! More than
that, Chelsie suddenly knew for sure that he was
articulate, cynical, unorthodox, and very probably
utterly brilliant, and that combination was far more
fatal than just a pretty face any day. She found herself
watching the subtle play of emotions that animated his
face. How odd that she could discern now what had
seemed concealed from her before. She could see
clearly that he was first amused and then merely bored
by his pretty companion's conversation.

She also felt a growing irritation with herself for
permitting this man to distract her so. He must be
aware of her and yet he showed no signs of it, and that
only irritated her further. She began to ask herself why

OF PASSION BORN   35

Andrew Bradford didn't just come up to her and say
whatever it was he had to say.

Instead, he seemed to be deliberately moving closer
and closer, subtly tightening the noose around her
neck. Chelsie was tempted to pretend she didn't
recognize him just in case he did dare to approach her.
But something told her that he would not be fooled for
one minute by that particular ploy.

She finally lost sight of her quarry. Or was *she* the
quarry? Moments later she had her answer. She knew
in some sixth-sense sort of way that Andrew Bradford
was directly behind her. She heard the familiar deep
timber of his voice as he greeted someone on the
fringe of their group and then caught a whiff of suede
and spicy aftershave. The skin on the back of Chelsie's
neck tingled. When she turned halfway around, she
found herself face to face with Andrew Bradford.

"Dr. McBride, I presume?" The man finally spoke,
the barest hint of a smile tugging at the edges of his
mouth.

Chelsie groaned inwardly. Oh, God, he was going
to have a sense of humor, too. She was such a sucker
for a man with a good sense of humor.

The young woman gave herself a good shake. "Yes,
I'm Dr. Chelsie McBride," she remarked with an
offhandedness she did not feel.

"Why didn't you tell me who you were this morning, Dr. McBride?" Andrew Bradford cut straight to
the heart of the matter.

"As I recall, *Professor* Bradford, we weren't exactly
in a position to exchange academic credentials,"
Chelsie replied with what she hoped was a casual air.

The man ran a hand through his attractive thatch of
dark brown hair. "Quite honestly, at the time of our

little run in, I had you pegged as a coed." He said the last as if it were a four-letter word of another kind.

"My first impression of you was that you were a boxer," she countered, equal to the occasion.

Andrew Bradford did not bother to disguise his surprise. "Do you like boxing, Dr. McBride?"

"I detest boxing!" she stated with the full force of her very real disapproval of the sport.

The man expelled a breath of indulgent laughter. "How fortunate for both of us then that our first impressions were so far from the truth. I'm not a boxer and you're not a silly young coed, after all."

Chelsie stood before him with her head thrown back, the clean line of her arched throat unintentionally inviting. "Yes—how fortunate," she agreed, only slightly mollified.

"You teach Chaucer?" Andrew Bradford continued with a discernible trace of irony in his voice.

"Yes, I do," she replied, trying to keep her tone from becoming defensive. "And what is your area of expertise, Professor Bradford?" Besides the obvious, she remarked to herself with a degree of cattiness.

"I'm a businessman, Dr. McBride. A businessman who decided to teach these kids something of the *real* world they'll encounter once they leave the protective walls of academia."

"You teach business?" Chelsie said innocently, employing Andrew Bradford's own form of address.

"I suppose you could say so," he replied, the faintest hint of scorn in his tone. "I like to think of it as more than that."

"I understand exactly what you mean," she hastened to explain, letting her eyes go wide. "Don't you think we all tend to pin simplified labels on what we try to do? I like to think that rather than just tutoring my students in the poetry of a man who lived in the Middle Ages, I help them to see the world a bit more clearly, to think for themselves."

"I have the strangest feeling I've just been told off," the man admitted with what sounded suspiciously like a chuckle.

Chelsie pursed her lips in satisfaction. "You're very quick, Professor Bradford."

"I try to live up to my reputation," he said, dangling the comment in front of her like a carrot.

All right, she would bite, thought Chelsie. "And what exactly is your reputation?" she murmured, knowing full well he had expected her to ask.

"That of a man who thinks on his feet," stated Andrew Bradford.

It wasn't the answer Chelsie McBride had expected, but then perhaps the man didn't *think* lying down.

"Ah—what evil little thoughts are going through that head of yours, Dr. McBride?" The color rose sharply in her face at his question. "By the way, is there a *Mister* McBride somewhere?" inquired her interrogator, while he had her on the spot.

"Several," she responded, rousing herself to this swift change of subject.

The man's features took on a judicial, appraising look. "You've been a busy girl. It would seem that I've misjudged you. I assumed your heart was in your work."

The perplexed expression on Chelsie's face finally dissolved as she realized the significance of Andrew Bradford's words. "It is. The several Mr. McBrides happen to be my older brothers. What about you, Professor?" she asserted. Turn about had always been fair play in Chelsie's book.

Andrew Bradford absently stroked his chin. "Hm—no brothers, I'm afraid. Or sisters either, for that matter," he answered with an obtuseness that fooled neither of them. "And no wife," he said at last, apparently tiring of that particular game.

Chelsie nearly added "but plenty of women," when the private nature of their conversation was altered by the arrival of the president of the college.

"I want to remind all of you that Mrs. Nelson and I are looking forward to seeing you at the faculty dinner dance on Friday evening," he announced to the group. Then Daniel Nelson zeroed in on Chelsie and the man standing beside her. "I see you and Drew have met, my dear."

"Yes—Professor Bradford and I were just discussing the various theories of education," Chelsie said blandly.

"Well, I'm sure that was most edifying for you both." Daniel Nelson had a dry wit that even he was unaware of at times. "I'm sure there are a number of your old friends here who would like to say hello to you, Chelsie. June and I will expect you on Friday, Drew." The man gave this last edict as he shook hands and began to move on to the the next group, expecting Chelsie to accompany him.

Andrew Bradford drew near for a moment and said, for her ears only, "I'd ask you to save a dance for me, Dr. McBride, but I'm wondering if you're any safer on the dance floor than you are on a bicycle."

Chelsie shook her head from side to side. "If I were you, Professor, I wouldn't take any chances. I've been known to knock 'em dead on the dance floor." Then she turned and accompanied Dr. Nelson on his rounds without so much as a glance back at Andrew Bradford.

In a cloud of swirling blue silk, Chelsie McBride was indeed out to "knock 'em dead" that Friday evening as she made her entrance at the country club with Lynn Marshall and her date.

"Now look you two, it was really very sweet of you to insist that I come with you, but I'm a big girl now and I don't want you thinking you have to hold my hand all evening," Chelsie lectured them gently.

"Don't be silly," scoffed Lynn, dismissing her friend's objections with a toss of her head. "Let's find ourselves a table and stake a claim to three places before it gets too crowded. There's an empty table over by the terrace. What do you think, Frank?"

The man at her side squared his shoulders and took charge as only an ex-football player can. "It looks good to me, Lynn. All right with you, Chelsie?"

"Sure!" She shrugged agreeably. "I wonder what we're having for dinner. I'm starved!"

"You aren't still subsisting on a diet of vanilla wafers, are you?" Lynn inquired with maternal concern.

"No," laughed Chelsie. "The next time you come over for coffee I can also offer you Fig Newtons."

"Fig Newtons! You have the strangest taste in food," said Lynn, as they trekked single file across the room.

Their conversation, half-serious, half-frivolous, carried them through the necessary introductions and small talk when another couple, the J. A. Hendersons —he in biology, she in home economics—joined them. It wasn't until she had downed a large crabmeat cocktail and was well into the beef stroganoff that Chelsie spotted Andrew Bradford at a table some distance from theirs.

For a moment she almost regretted the unobstructed view she had of him, then she gave in to a grudging admiration of the dark blue suit he was wearing—no doubt the work of a tailor, judging by the way it fit his broad shoulders to a T. His crisp white shirt contrasted sharply with the healthy tan he sported. A tan he had acquired, she supposed, while out doing all that jogging in the park.

Blue was certainly Andrew Bradford's color—and he knew it, too, she guessed. But since when had it been a sin for a man to know what looked good on him? Hadn't she purposely worn the blue silk for that very reason herself? Chelsie took one last note of Professor Andrew Bradford's appearance and then deliberately avoided looking in that direction again. It was, after all, a simple matter of self-preservation.

Quite honestly, Chelsie never considered the possibility of feeling like a fifth wheel until dinner was over and the dance band began to move into place. Then she suddenly found herself rather awkwardly the odd man out. There sat Lynn and Frank and the Hendersons—she could have sworn with toes a-tapping—but because they had either to take turns on the dance floor or leave Chelsie on her own, no one made a move.

"Well—" she finally said, fixing an expression of bright enthusiasm on her face, "I see a number of old acquaintances I really should say hello to. So if you don't mind," she took a quick survey of those around the table, ". . . I think I'll be off! See you all later," she called back over one shoulder before merging into the crowd gathered at the bar at one end of the room.

Chelsie took a deep breath to fortify herself and slipped into the first powder room she came to. If for no other reason than to kill a little time, she leisurely checked her hair and makeup before venturing forth again.

The problem, she thought as she purposely strolled across the room toward the open terrace doors, was that the world had always been one of couples—two-by-two—since the time of Noah's Ark. The state of being a single woman was one she had accepted long ago, but there were the odd moments every now and then when Chelsie felt a pang of regret, of loneliness, she supposed, that there was no one special man in her life. She wouldn't be human if she didn't feel that way sometimes.

Absorbed as she was in her work and in the circle of friends she had at Bryn Mawr, and having her fair share of light romantic interests, there were still times when Chelsie McBride wondered if the right man would ever come along. She wasn't holding her breath or anything. In fact, she wasn't sure such a man existed. But in that secretmost part of herself, she sometimes admitted to a terrible loneliness—a loneliness for the experiences every woman dreams of, hopes will be hers, with a man who loves her.

It was entirely possible that she would never experience the mature version of the teenage crush she had had on Gerry Marshall at sixteen. Good men were hard to find even if a woman was looking—and Chelsie wasn't looking.

Really—this mood is ridiculous, she laughed to

herself. She had simply left the table for a few minutes to allow the others a chance to dance without feeling they were leaving her out. She was being silly—helped along by two glasses of Cabernet Sauvignon, her absolute limit on most occasions.

But the evening was a rare one, she acknowledged as she stepped out onto the terrace. A slight breeze rolled a few crisp brown leaves along the walk below. Autumn was fast approaching—the season of smoky fires and goose bumps in the morning as one ran to close the bedroom window, and the glorious transformation of the world from green to gold and scarlet and bright yellow.

Chelsie knew people who found autumn depressing, who saw it as the end of the year rather than the best of a continuous cycle, as she preferred to think of it. She drew in a breath of fresh air that still had the aroma of summer clinging to it and remarked to herself that it was a glorious night.

"Hello, Chelsie." The voice behind her was full and strong, accustomed to command.

It was also the first time she could recall Andrew Bradford using her given name.

"Hello," she remarked in return, without turning her head. The silence grew between them until it got on Chelsie's nerves. "Lovely evening," she finally said, not moving.

"Yes, it is a lovely evening, isn't it?" he concurred, as he came to stand beside her.

"I just felt like being by myself," she offered as an explanation for her absence from the party.

A sardonic expression crept over Andrew Bradford's features. "Would you like me to leave?" It wasn't asked out of anger, but with some gruffness nonetheless.

Chelsie made a quick, involuntary movement with her hands. "Oh, no, I—I didn't mean it like that, Andrew." His name slipped effortlessly from her lips as she hastened to reassure him he was welcome.

"Then I'll stay—if you promise to dance with me, Dr. McBride," he said, with a carefully straight face.

"But the band has stopped playing . . . there isn't any music," she pointed out.

A grin appeared on his face. "How can you say that when you've never heard me hum?" He pretended to ignore the slight.

Chelsie looked at him askance. "Won't the others think it a little odd?"

"Do you always worry about what other people will think?" he accused her with a sweeping generalization.

She was just as quick to defend herself. "Almost never."

"Well, neither do I—but if it will make you feel any better, I doubt if we can be seen from inside." He opened his arms wide in invitation. "May I have the honor of this dance, Chelsie McBride? And please, call me Drew. No one calls me Andrew."

It was Chelsie's first contact with the hard, muscular male body since she had searched Andrew Bradford for injuries that day in the park. Her mouth went suddenly dry, as it had the night of her first school dance when she was a girl of thirteen. There was the same sense of expectancy, the same butterflies— though she was a little older and wiser—in the pit of her stomach. She was quite sure, however, that if this man took her home from the dance, it would take more than a little handholding to satisfy him. But then she was beyond the innocent handholding stage herself.

Chelsie moved self-consciously into his arms as Drew did indeed begin to hum some nameless romantic tune in her ear. He had a very pleasant voice, but it was utterly impossible to relax under the circumstances. She knew she was moving awkwardly—but she felt rather ridiculous.

"Relax, Chelsie," he murmured, drawing her closer.

Then the band must have returned from their break, for a haunting melody seemed to float out through the open doors just for them.

Chelsie found herself caught up in the song—always one of her favorites—and the next thing she knew she had totally relaxed against the man, the length of her body pressed to his. From the top of her forehead, which rested against his chin, to the curve of her thigh, which brushed along his leg, she was aware of the way they moved together.

It was as if their bodies acknowledged an intimacy between them that each of them would have been reluctant to put into words. And it was true in a way that the best things happen while dancing. Chelsie lost her self-consciousness as they swayed and stepped through song after song emanating from inside the country club.

It was one of those nights full of magic and make believe. A velvet-black night without a touch of reality. It reminded Chelsie of a scene from the movie "White Christmas"—the one where Danny Kaye and Vera Ellen dance out onto a terrace and fall in love.

"What are you thinking about?" Drew said in a deceptively mild tone.

"What skinny legs Vera Ellen had!" she answered after an interval.

At this he really laughed, but much to Chelsie's surprise he did not say "who the hell is Vera Ellen?" In fact, he sounded suddenly quite human. "Hm . . . good dancer, but you're right about the skinny legs."

"I always wanted to be able to dance like that." She confessed her childhood dreams in a whisper. "But as a young girl I danced like an elephant in a snowdrift, according to my older brothers."

"Those would be the several Mr. McBrides you mentioned on a previous occasion?"

"Yes, the very same," she smiled.

"Well, don't feel too bad—you've got it over Vera Ellen any day when it comes to legs." Drew ran his hand down her thigh in a caressing assessment. "Not too skinny, either," he said, with a glint of satisfaction in his eye.

Chelsie knew then that Drew Bradford wanted to kiss her, that he intended to kiss her. It was there in his eyes and in the way his hand moved in small sensual circles along her hip. She was equally curious about him, so when his mouth found hers it seemed the most natural thing in the world to kiss him back.

It wasn't true, of course, that most men knew how to kiss. Chelsie had run into her share of overconfident amateurs through the years. But Drew's kiss was light and sweet-tasting, and she found she rather liked it. She moved closer to him, letting her arms fall from his shoulders to his waist where they snaked around under his coat.

She awoke from the dream to realize that the kiss

between them was no longer a simple, sweet exploration. It was fast becoming a force with the power to
explode out of control. Chelsie had no wish to lead
this man on to think of her as easy, but for once in her
life—well, perhaps more than once—she decided to
live dangerously.

When Drew decided to put more of himself into
what had obviously become some kind of experiment,
Chelsie joined in. He coaxed her further into the
shadows as his mouth drew her into a spiraling
darkness of its own. She could not see her way, only
feel the mesmerizing addiction of his lips. He tasted
better than any man she had ever kissed—not with
any artificial breath sweetener, just the natural taste of
him. It was distinctly Drew, she knew that.

Then the explosion came, as Chelsie had half-
feared, half-hoped it would. His hands stroked the
length of her back and down over the rounded curves
of her bottom until he felt compelled to cup and lift her
against him. In a simultaneous assault, his mouth
teased and tormented hers until with a groan Chelsie
opened her lips to his tongue.

It was certainly not the first time a man had kissed
her in such a manner. After all, she was a twenty-
eight-year-old woman, not some post-pubescent teenager. But what Chelsie could not begin to explain was
her own reaction to Drew's touch. She was all
atremble from her sun-streaked hair down to her toes,
toes that insisted upon curling up in the oddest
fashion. She was good and truly caught in the grip of a
pure physical passion such as she had not known
herself capable of.

And it seemed that Drew Bradford found himself to
be in a similar state—for as his roving hands and lips

sampled the delights of her body and skin, lost themselves in the silky sheen of her hair, his own body reacted like that of an overeager adolescent. She could sense the hunger in him, the aroused passion.

When he finally drew away from her, Chelsie could have sworn there was the faintest tint of red in his tanned face. Then he laughed unexpectedly and uncomfortably.

"I must apologize, Dr. McBride, for my apparent lack of control." His gray eyes narrowed in thought. "I—ah can't really explain what happened." Drew rubbed one hand along the back of his neck. "Hell, Chelsie—at my age a man kisses an attractive woman for the first time more out of curiosity than passion."

She drew in a shaky breath. The silly man! She wasn't insulted by what had happened. If anything, she was flattered, even elated.

"You don't have to explain or apologize, you know." Chelsie raised her hand to his face where the strong outline of his jaw was rigid beneath her touch. One step took her to within an inch of him. She took her hand away as her lips claimed the spot on his cheek that had been warmed by her caress. "I like the way you kiss very much, Professor Bradford." Then Chelsie kissed him full on the lips—not as a tease would, but in a straightforward manner that clearly said she found him attractive—*all* of him.

When her kiss was completed, Drew continued to casually hold her within the circle of his arms as he gazed down into her face. "I don't usually ask a woman to go to bed on the first date—at least I haven't since I was a kid—but God, woman, I'd like to take you home with me!"

There was an odd little silence. "This isn't a first

date. It isn't a date at all," Chelsie said quietly, undoing her hand from his.

Drew merely smiled and shrugged. "Then what would the eminent doctor prescribe for this strange fever?"

"Well. . . ." Chelsie moistened her bottom lip.

"No—don't tell me!" He took advantage of her hesitancy and spoke first. "Take two aspirin and call in the morning, right?"

She concealed a smile. "As I said before, Professor Bradford—you're very quick."

"Apparently not quick enough . . . this time," he muttered under his breath. "You win, Dr. McBride! I concede round one to you. But take heed—I promise to come out fighting like a pro in the next round."

As they walked side by side back into the country club, Chelsie McBride couldn't help wondering when the bell would sound on round two and just how on earth she was to combat Drew Bradford now that he had made up his mind to be the victor in their match.

3

~~~~~~~~~~~~~~~~

Hunting often suggested a sexual escapade in medieval literature," Dr. Chelsie McBride stated in her best professorial voice. She stepped away from the podium at the front of the lecture hall and continued, "The *hare,* for example, was and still is a symbol of lechery." She gave the class one of her knowing smiles. "I knew that would get your attention."

"Look for the animal references as you read *The Canterbury Tales,* keeping in mind Chaucer's sometimes rather earthy sense of humor. I'm sure that won't be difficult for this class," she said, ribbing the rather large roomful of students with its disproportionate number of young men. She had been told the class size would be limited to thirty, but as usual enrollment seemed to be double that.

Chelsie paused for a moment to pick up her well-thumbed copy of Chaucer. "The next time this class meets we will be discussing the "Miller's Tale." Be prepared for the bawdy humor in this one. The author himself warns his readers of its content. Just to whet your appetites, let me read you a small portion of the 'Miller's Tale.' "

But as she opened her mouth to read, Chelsie happened to glance up and behold, with a slight squint, a familiar figure at the back of the classroom. Damn! Could it really be Drew Bradford? she asked herself unhappily, as she made a small production of returning to the podium for her glasses.

Actually, Chelsie only needed her glasses for driving, but she somehow felt more in command of herself behind their large frames. She slipped them on and proceeded to make a surreptitious sweep of the room, affirming that it was indeed Drew Bradford sitting there looking for all the world as though her every word was of immense interest to him.

That was all it took to unnerve her. She fumbled the pages for a moment, temporarily losing her place. "Ah—as I was saying, let me read you an excerpt from the 'Miller's Tale,' in the original Middle English:

> She was a primerole, a piggesnye
> For any lord to leggen in his bedde,
> Or yet for any good yeman to wedde.

I hope the English of Chaucer's time is becoming easier for you to read, so you could understand that excerpt. Until our next class then. . . ." She abruptly dismissed the class, dismayed that Drew Bradford's sudden appearance should have embarrassed her.

Oh, great God! Chelsie moaned to herself. She was

neither an easily titillated teenager nor a middle-aged prude. There were all kinds of references to sex in the great literature she taught. It was as natural as the rising and setting of the sun. She was simply not going to allow this man to get to her again. He had done enough of that already in the brief span of their acquaintanceship. Nevertheless, Chelsie made very sure she was busy sorting papers and books as Andrew Bradford came down the center aisle toward her.

She had not seen him since the dinner dance at the country club the previous Friday evening. She hadn't known quite what to expect of a man like Drew after their encounter on the terrace and so she had expected nothing. That way she had only thought once or twice over the weekend that he might call.

"Hello, Chelsie!" There it was again—that voice that immediately put her on red alert.

She called forth the greater part of her defenses and managed to return the greeting with the same degree of nonchalance. "Oh—hello, Drew."

"I enjoyed the lecture." He seemed almost surprised that he had. "Now that I've heard your interpretation of the old boy, I may just have to read Chaucer again."

Chelsie stood a little straighter. "I'm glad you found my class so enlightening, Professor Bradford."

"Oh, I did indeed, Dr. McBride," he said, looking casually intrigued. "I learned a great deal from your class." But Chelsie had the funniest feeling that he was not referring to either Chaucer or *The Canterbury Tales*. Drew went on with a crooked smile, "Did you miss me this weekend?"

"Were you gone?" Chelsie replied airily.

"Yes, I was gone. Why do you think I didn't call you?" he informed her with his own brand of easy grace.

"Were you planning to call me?" she inquired, as if his answer made not the slightest difference to her.

Drew Bradford brushed an impatient hand across his forehead. "Yes, I was planning to, but I got an urgent business call early Saturday and had to fly to Albany for the weekend. I just got back this morning," he explained, as if explanations were definitely something out of the ordinary for him.

"How nice for you," murmured Chelsie, as she continued with the business of gathering up her materials in preparation for her imminent departure.

"Hell, no, it wasn't nice for me! I wanted to see you again, Chelsie." Drew moved in closer, taking her glasses as he spoke and depriving her of one of her much needed defenses in the process. "You know, Dr. McBride, beneath that rather stuffy academicism you're just the slightest bit bawdy yourself." He took the final step toward her, making any evasive action next to impossible. He stood planted in front of her like one of the silent giants of Stonehenge. "How about having lunch with me?"

Chelsie paused with her hand in midair. "I—ah. . . ."

"I've already checked your schedule. You don't have any classes this afternoon," he said, effectively cutting off that avenue of retreat.

"Really, Drew, I—" she groped for the right words.

"I'll pick you up at Mrs. Freeman's in an hour. And dress casually—it's a very informal place," he said, suppressing a grin.

A look of vexation passed over Chelsie McBride's face. "How did you know I live at Esther Freeman's?"

Something flickered behind his eyes. Then he laughed. A long, rich, deep laugh. "The secretary in personnel was very cooperative."

Chelsie made a disparaging sound. "I'll just bet she was!"

"I'd walk you to your car, but I have an advisory meeting with a student in exactly—" Drew glanced down at the silver-banded Seiko on his wrist, "two and a half minutes."

"I think I can manage without you," stated Chelsie, fully intending him to interpret the double-entendre as just that. She collected her briefcase and turned to leave. "May I have my glasses now, please?"

"Of course! We wouldn't want you running down any innocent pedestrians on the way home, would we?" He slipped the glasses around each ear and gently settled them on the bridge of Chelsie's nose. "I'll see you in one hour, honey. Be ready!" Then Drew swooped down and took a hard, swift bite of her breath with his kiss.

Chelsie was still sputtering when she surfaced from the impact of his arrogant mouth, but Drew was already out the door of the classroom. She gave the room one final check before switching off the over-head lights and heading for her car. But she couldn't shake the feeling that the bell had rung on round two!

Chelsie was ready and sitting on the front steps of the Freeman house five minutes before the hour was up. Despite Andrew Bradford's overbearing attitude about their luncheon date, she found the prospect of going out with the man irresistible. And while she was changing, Chelsie had faced the fact that she found the *man* irresistible, as well. He was so many things she admired—intelligent, articulate, funny. She could almost forgive him the occasional arrogance that tended to surface when he didn't get his own way. She supposed that had more to do with the hard-boiled businessman than the erudite college professor.

She cradled her chin in her hands, elbows propped on khaki gabardine pants, and absently studied a caravan of red ants trudging from one side of the walk to the other. It was scarcely several minutes past the appointed hour when she looked up to see Drew Bradford coming down the street.

Chelsie's mouth dropped open in amazement. Then she burst out in unrestrained giggles. As he came up the drive, she made a valiant effort to stifle her mirth, but to no avail.

"Oh, Drew—" she choked as she got to her feet, two tears starting a slow path down her cheeks. "I don't believe this—a bicycle built for two!"

He leaned the tandem against the porch, caught his breath for a moment, and then spoke. "I figured it would be impossible for you to run into me if we were on the same bicycle."

"Well, I must say I admire a man who doesn't hold a grudge," Chelsie grinned, still shaking her head in disbelief. "But where do you intend to take me on this thing?"

With a flourish of his hand, Drew indicated the picnic hamper strapped to the front of the two-wheeled contraption. "We are going to the park for a picnic, Dr. McBride. If that meets with your approval."

"It does," she replied, in the spirit of good fun.

The man eyed her up and down, apparently taking note of the khaki shirt and pants and her utilitarian loafers. "I see you've dressed for the occasion as I instructed." Drew seemed almost smug about it.

Chelsie acquiesced with a shrug. "I took you at your word, Professor Bradford. I assume you mean what you say," she added with spirit.

"I did in this case," he said, noncommittally, turning away to retrieve the bicycle. "You take the front seat," he ordered. "I'll bring up the aft."

"I'd prefer to ride in back," she stated, realizing that if she sat in front it would give him an unrestricted view of her backside.

"No way—" Drew said. He turned to Chelsie and firmly brought her face up to his. "Not that I don't trust you, sweetheart, but I want you in my sights at all times." Then he gave her a resounding kiss on the mouth, apparently unconcerned that they were in a public place.

Her argument so dispensed with, Chelsie mounted the bicycle and at Drew's command they pushed off together, heading down Ivy Place toward one of the side entrances to Wilber Park. With only an occasional barked order from Drew, they managed to pedal along the paved road almost in unison.

It was one of those rare days caught between summer and fall. The sky was so blue it nearly caused one's breath to catch at its unmarred beauty. The world was still a kelly green, but there was a harbinger here and there along the way of the changes that would soon take place.

Chelsie had thought she knew every nook and cranny of Wilber Park, but she was quickly to learn that there were intimate little spots all over the large grounds that she was unaware of. They had traversed the low ground and were headed up the big hill when Drew shouted out to turn right ahead. This was almost immediately followed by "slow down," and finally a rather perfunctory "stop."

They had stopped by a secluded grove of pine trees in a section of the park Chelsie was unfamiliar with. They dismounted and stood there for a moment to regain their land legs.

"I thought I knew every inch of this park," she mused, "but I don't remember this place."

"That's right—you used to live in Oneonta, didn't you?" said Drew, as he unstrapped the hamper. He took Chelsie by the hand and guided her toward a warm, sunny patch of grass between the tall trees.

"Yes—" Chelsie murmured rather absently. "I grew up here, as a matter of fact. We lived in a big gray and white house with cherry-red doors. Right down there on East Street. Do you know that after all this time the people living there still have those doors painted the same shade of red? I used to spend a lot of time in this park. When I was a teenager they held dances on the tennis courts in the summer. They would string Christmas lights all along the wire enclosures and play the standard rock hits over a loudspeaker. We'd dance and drink cokes. . . ."

". . . and steal away into the night," Drew finished for her.

"Yes—" she smiled nostalgically, "sometimes we would steal away into the night. I've been away from Oneonta for more than a decade, but I've never forgotten it. I think that of all the places I've lived this is still my favorite. A small city with most of the amenities of a much larger one."

"Why don't we sit down while we stroll down memory lane?" Drew grinned, extracting an old army blanket that had been secured to the top of the picnic hamper. "Here—you take that end," he suggested. They managed on the second try to spread the blanket out straight.

"I'm sorry, Drew. I didn't mean to bore you. As a matter of fact, I'm not usually the sentimental type. Somehow coming here now has unleashed so many memories for me. I suppose none of us forgets the place where we first fell in love . . . our first date, the first car. So many firsts happened to me here, you see." Chelsie looked at him for some kind of confirmation that he did indeed understand and perhaps wasn't even bored.

"I'm not in the least bored," he said, stretching out on the blanket beside her. "But I don't believe in looking back myself. Nothing is ever accomplished by dwelling on what once was." Something in his tone made Chelsie glance at him, but his expression told her nothing.

"It's not that I'm trying to accomplish anything by it," she explained, after it was apparent he was not going to continue, "but it does help me understand how I became the woman I am today. This town is very much a part of me."

Suddenly Drew's tanned face dissolved into a smile. "In that case, I say *bravo* to Oneonta, New York! They sure did something right."

Chelsie rather liked that smile on his face and decided a change of subject was the best way for her to see it again. "Gosh, with all the talking I've been doing, I've really worked up an appetite!"

"Is that synonymous with 'when do we eat?'" Drew

asked, and she responded with an eager nod. "My, my, you have such a way with words, Dr. McBride!"

"You did say this was a date for lunch," she chose to remind him.

"So I did," he admitted with what sounded suspiciously like a chuckle. Drew opened the lid of the picnic basket and peered inside as though he had never seen the thing before. "Let's see what dear Edith packed for our lunch, then, shall we?"

One gracefully arched brow rose questioningly. "Edith?"

"Edith Sawyer—my housekeeper. You surely didn't think I threw this little repast together in my spare time, did you? My proficiency in the kitchen doesn't extend beyond a peanut butter and jelly sandwich." The grimace on Drew Bradford's handsome face said it all.

"In a real pinch, I've been known to eat peanut butter and jelly sandwiches three nights in a row," Chelsie said with an exaggerated sigh.

Drew gave her slender figure a long, searching examination. "It doesn't seem to have done any permanent damage," he said in a dry tone. "I can assure you, however, that Edith Sawyer's culinary skills go beyond mere sandwiches. That's why I hired her."

He proceeded to prove his point by extracting from the hamper an assortment of delicacies that ranged from the best cold boneless chicken Chelsie had ever tasted to light French pastries that literally melted in her mouth. In between they managed to sample a superb cucumber and shrimp salad and a spicy concoction of chilled vegetables, all washed down with a choice of either cold beer or sparkling bottled water.

Completely satiated, Chelsie lay back on the blanket and found herself a shady spot where the sun did not touch her skin. She felt rather than saw Drew stretch out beside her. For a moment she held her breath in expectation, wondering if he would make some move toward her. When he failed to do so she turned toward him, propping her head on her arm. Drew lay there, eyes wide open, staring at some distant point she was unable to discern.

"I don't know very much about you, you know," she murmured, noting the way the snug jeans fit his rock-hard thighs.

Drew Bradford turned his gray-green eyes in her direction. "What exactly did you want to know?"

"How like a man," she smiled. "You tell him practically your whole life story over lunch and you don't even know how tall he is."

"Five eleven," he stated.

This gave Chelsie pause. "Huh?" she grunted inelegantly.

"I'm five feet eleven inches tall," Drew repeated.

"Now that's more like it!" Her blue eyes flickered with humor. "You are just under six feet tall, a businessman cum college professor, and, according to unreliable sources, not married." Chelsie ticked the points off on her fingers. "What more could I possibly need to know?"

Without warning Drew sprang into action, pinning her beneath him in one fluid movement of his body. "That sharp tongue of yours is going to get you into serious trouble one day, Chelsie McBride."

Her skin glowed, warm and rich, like silk as his weight pressed her into the hard ground beneath the flimsy blanket. "Tell me about it," she dared him.

"So you want to know something about me, do

you?" Drew punctuated the question with a swift, hard kiss to her lips. "I am thirty-seven years old and definitely not married." He repeated the action a second time with even greater insistence. "Until a year ago I was president of Bradford Electronics. Corporate offices located in Albany, New York. I resigned that position, but retain a seat on the board of directors." His third kiss was lingering, less harsh, less motivated by retribution than the others. In fact, he seemed to be losing his train of thought—and willingly, at that. "I've—I have been teaching business courses here at Oneonta for the past twelve months and up until a few days ago led a very comfortable existence."

Then he came to her a fourth time, lingering over her mouth, relishing the warmth and sweetness of it that contrasted with the piquancy of her darting tongue as it imitated his in exploration of moist, dark places. This kiss was thorough. It was everything a kiss should be—driving, demanding, bittersweet to the point of tears. Chelsie was intensely aware of his vibrant body pressing against her, the long line of his thighs contoured to her own softer form. She felt her passion rise like a phoenix from the ashes of indifference.

His kiss had been intended as a chastisement, but as he withdrew his mouth from Chelsie's they both knew the lesson learned had been of an entirely different nature.

"That'll teach you to curb that tongue of yours," Drew exhaled in a strange, husky voice—a voice that betrayed him as surely as his body had.

"Is this method of instruction one you often use, Professor?" Chelsie managed to ask in a near normal tone.

"Only in extreme cases, Dr. McBride." The mocking look was back in his eyes. "You are one stubborn woman."

"I am not!" she protested.

If the spark of combat in the gray depths of his eyes had not warned her, the purposeful intent of his body would have. "You'll never learn, will you?" Drew's head thrust forward suddenly as he moved in for the kill.

There was a moment of fear interlaced with intense desire as Chelsie realized Drew had every intention of kissing her again. He obviously felt that she needed to be taught a lesson and that he was the man to do it. She even tried to convince herself it would take a bigger man than Andrew Bradford, but a nagging suspicion warned her that all five feet eleven inches of him were lethal.

Then his lips were grinding into hers, alternately punishing and making retribution, first taking and then giving, hard and soft, ice and fire, until her senses were reeling with the wild gamut of emotions he was proving could be hers. Then, as before, the intent of the lesson subtly shifted until they were above all else a man and a woman finding pleasure in each other.

And such a passionate pleasure it was! He gently closed her eyes with his lips, nipped at the tender lobe of her ear with teeth that teased her, buried his face in the silky fragrance of her hair—touching, tasting, smelling. But he was not alone. He robbed Chelsie of her breath, only to have her steal it back again.

Chelsie had never been one to stand back and let a man do all the work—or have all the fun. She joined in with all the sweet desire that surged through her and bubbled to the surface like fine champagne. Her mouth opened and moved and ultimately moaned its pleasure beneath his. Her fingertips trickled down his body, touching the sensitive skin below an ear, the tensed muscles in the back of his neck, the soft mat of dark hair.

Groaning unintelligibly, Drew wrapped his strong arms around her. Her own clung to his neck as they rolled over and over in tandem, landing in a bed of sweet-scented grass. For an instant Chelsie was aware of each individual blade pricking her back through the cotton shirt. Then Drew was kissing her, touching her, and all other sensations were forgotten.

For the first time in her life she realized her breasts were throbbing, yearning, aching for a man's touch. If she and Drew had been lovers, she would boldly have placed his hands on her, asking for the pleasure they could bring.

As though he read her mind, or perhaps acting in response to some driving need of his own, Drew concentrated his attention at last on the twin peaks that strained against her shirt like two hard buttons. He cupped one breast in his palm, seemingly amazed at the way it spilled over into his hand. Then he repeated the process with the other breast, as if to reassure himself that their inviting fullness was not a figment of his imagination.

Passion-filled eyes studied her face as his deft fingers released the buttons down the front of her shirt, one by one. As the front closure of her bra was undone, exposing her bare flesh to Drew's gaze, Chelsie felt a warm breeze caress her skin.

She waited for the abrasive touch she knew would come and when it did it set off a series of small explosions inside her. With practiced ease, Drew flicked the erect nipple with his finger, watching as it responded to his manipulation by becoming still harder.

The same probing, penetrating tongue that had ravished her mouth now sought to sample and savor other secrets. The neglected bud was caught between his teeth while the other was rolled between finger and thumb. The dual assault was more than Chelsie could bear. She arched her body toward Drew's, groaning his name over and over in passionate anguish. A sharp pain born of pleasure snaked down her body until it centered itself in the very core of her being.

Her fingers and mind aquiver with passion, Chelsie sought to unbutton Drew's shirt. His body was taut beneath her touch, the flesh firm, the muscles contracted with tension. Her lips found his skin surprisingly smooth and soft as she rained a string of kisses across his chest. The mat of dark hair with an occasional silver thread running through it tickled her nose as she nuzzled against him.

Seeking to know more of her, Drew ran a caressing hand down her slender form from throat to thigh, then let his hand travel inward to find the sensitive vee where her legs met. A groan of suppressed desire came from them both in unison. They burned with a thirst for each other that only the complete union of their bodies would quench. They were not two young kids discovering sex for the first time, but a mature man and woman who wanted each other in the most elemental way a man and woman can.

Just at the point of no return, Drew backed off and struggled to regain his self-control. "My God, woman,

I want to make love to you so badly I forgot where we are!" He rolled away from her and lay there for a moment, his breath coming erratically. Then he turned and gently pulled her disheveled clothing into some semblance of order. "Every time I get near you, Chelsie McBride, I lose control of myself," he muttered gutturally. "I said it the first time we met, not knowing then how true it was—you are a dangerous young woman!" There was no anger directed at her in his voice, only impatience with himself.

It was a full minute before Chelsie could speak. Her blue eyes approached the color of midnight, darkened by the emotions she was still struggling to contain. Her skin glowed with a rosy hue, not just on her face, but everywhere.

She inhaled a slow, trembling breath. "When it comes to being dangerous, I'm a rank amateur compared to you, Drew Bradford!" Knowing he was watching her every move with something akin to regret, she quickly completed the process of putting her clothes in order. Then she knelt in front of him and began to do up the buttons of his shirt.

Drew caught her hands in his, staying their movement. His eyes burned like coals. "You know I want you, honey—and I think you want me as well. We can go our separate ways now before it's too late, or take a chance—because if we go on seeing each other we both know that sooner or later we're going to end up lovers."

The color rose sharply in her face. "I'd really rather not talk about it, Drew."

He caught hold of her unceremoniously by the shoulders. "We have to talk about it, Chelsie. We're not a couple of kids rushing into a one-night stand. At my age I'm not a man of promiscuous tastes, but neither do I believe that an affair must necessarily mean a lifelong commitment." He paused and then said in a different voice, "It's been years—maybe never—since I've wanted a woman as I want you. I want you in the physical sense, yes, but I also admire the mind inside that body. The choice is still ours, Chelsie, both of ours. But it may not always be that way since it's pretty obvious I can't keep my hands off you. I know the time will come when I won't even want to try." He stopped as if he had run out of breath. "Dammit, woman, don't you realize what it cost me to say that when some primitive instinct tells me to simply throw you over my shoulder and carry you off?"

Chelsie was startled by his outburst at first, then she saw the humor in it, as she always managed somehow to find humor in things. "Then *bravo,* professor, I applaud your higher instincts!" She bit the corners of her mouth against a smile. "You know, appearances can be so deceptive—on be surface you seem quite civilized."

Drew's forehead creased a moment perplexedly. Then he gave an indignant grunt as though he wasn't sure if he had been praised or insulted. "I have always thought of myself as a civilized man," he stated with a hint of pomposity.

That struck some maternal chord in Chelsie. She could suddenly see quite clearly the ten-year-old boy in the man. "Oh, Drew Bradford, I do love you!" she exclaimed with a laugh, throwing her arms about his neck. Then she realized the sensual interpretation he had put on her action and words and quickly drew back. "Wait—I—I didn't mean it like that, Drew. It's just that. . . ." She stammered to a halt, then tried again. "What I meant was I *like* you," she corrected herself, her arms dropping to her sides.

But the gleam in his eye told her it was too late as Drew swept away this last consideration with a wave of his hand. "I can only assume, Dr. McBride, that you say what you mean."

"I have already explained, I meant 'I love you' in the sense of 'I like you,'" she groaned, a little exasperated.

The man gave an indifferent shrug. "If you say so, honey."

"And that's another thing," she snapped. "My name is Chelsie, not *honey!*"

"My—my—you are all hot and bothered, aren't you?" Drew teased. "What you need is a nice cool swim and I know just the place where you can get one."

Chelsie flung up her defiant chin. "Oh, sure—where?" she asked, trying to curb her irritation. For a day in early September it had gotten surprisingly hot and a swim did sound very attractive.

"I know of a house nearby with a lovely pool just waiting to be used."

"Are you saying that your house is around here somewhere and you have a swimming pool?" she asked point blank.

"You're very quick, Dr. McBride," said Drew, with a carefully straight face. "Do I take it your answer is yes?"

Chelsie bit her lip as she accepted the hand he

extended to her. "Yes—my answer is yes," she finally said.

But as they prepared to leave the park for his home, Chelsie realized a distant church bell was chiming three o'clock and she wondered if it were at all wise to risk going another round with Drew Bradford so soon.

4

~~~ecececececec~~~

They had pedaled for a number of blocks, mostly uphill, when Chelsie felt compelled to register a complaint with Drew. In the first place, she was hot and sticky with perspiration and in the second, her leg muscles were beginning to ache from the strenuous exercise.

"I thought you said your house was nearby," she called over one shoulder in an accusatory tone.

"It is . . . on foot." She could detect the laughter in Drew's voice. "Well, you could hardly expect us to cut cross-country on this contraption," he called to her.

Several minutes later, after a series of hairpin turns that had Chelsie completely lost, he indicated that they were finally there.

"Turn left at the next street," he directed.

They found themselves following a tree-lined driveway of sorts, and then ahead and off to one side of the road a rustic cabin came into view.

It wasn't at all what Chelsie had expected—not that she had known what to expect, really—but she did concede the surprise was a pleasant one.

"Oh, Drew—it's enchanting!" she whispered fervently, taking an immediate liking to the roughly hewn house that nestled snugly in a grove of towering fir trees. A screened-in porch ran the entire forty-foot length of the large square cabin. The grounds were landscaped with native plantings. In surroundings like these one could almost forget how close at hand civilization was, she mused, as they parked the bicycle by a small storage shed.

Drew slung the picnic hamper over one arm and threw his other casually around Chelsie's shoulders.

"C'mon, honey—this way," he said, with a nod of his handsome head, apparently forgetting her rather vehement objection to his use of that particular endearment.

Passing through the front door of the cabin, Chelsie exhaled an exclamation of delight. For there in front of her was a room of immense proportions. Her first impression was one of primitive yet elegant decor. A massive stone hearth and fireplace took up one end of the room. Rustic log walls had been left exposed on three sides of the cabin, and the fourth was a wall of glass. A natural wood-beamed ceiling peaked high overhead and an open stairway led to a second-story loft above. And there were bookcases everywhere! The room had a luxurious but lived-in look to it.

The earth-tone color scheme retained the authentic flavor of the cabin, with an occasional bright patch of red here and there to relieve the monotony. The secondary color had been effectively used in the throw pillows on the twin love seats before the fireplace and in the chair pads in the dining area, and then was picked up again in the braided rugs that were scattered about on the plank floor.

Literally dozens of oil paintings and watercolors adorned the walls, the most impressive directly over the fireplace mantel, all highlighted by several large wooden chandeliers that hung on chains from the high peaked ceiling.

Drew took giant strides across the room to the kitchen alcove, setting the picnic basket down on the counter.

"Would you like something to drink?" he inquired, opening the door of the refrigerator before she could answer. "I have just about everything on tap."

"I'd love it!" Chelsie replied, her thirst coming back to haunt her at the mere mention of a cold drink. She claimed one of the stools at the counter for her own and watched as Drew examined the contents of his well-stocked refrigerator.

"I can offer you beer, wine, iced tea, soft drinks, or a nonalcoholic piña colada over crushed ice. I talked a friend of mine in the fast-drink business out of the recipe for that one. It's delicious if you like exotic drinks."

"It sounds heavenly. I'll have a piña colada."

Chelsie watched as Drew took out a blender, poured pineapple juice into it and added some kind of powder, followed by crushed ice. He gave it a whirl and poured the light, frothy drink into two tall glasses, setting one in front of her. She took a tentative sip before pronouncing judgment.

"My compliments to your friend. This is really very good!" she said, taking a long, cool draught of the fruity drink. Observing that the kitchen had every modern convenience known to man, and that no expense had been spared in the decoration of the cabin, Chelsie remarked, "You sure didn't buy this place on a professor's salary."

Drew gave the room behind her a cursory examination. "I don't own the cabin. I'm renting it until I decide if I want to stay here at Oneonta."

"There's a chance you won't?" she asked, curiosity getting the best of her.

"A good chance." He stared down into his half-empty glass. "I've only been teaching a year now, Chelsie. I have been involved with Bradford Electronics in one way or another all my life. It's in my blood. I don't know yet if I can walk away from it with no regrets." Drew stopped long enough to refill their glasses and take a seat on the stool beside her.

"At twenty-three, with a dual degree in history and business, I wanted nothing more than to teach. My father was president of the firm then. He spent a lot of nights over a lot of scotch and waters talking me into coming with the company. He felt I had too good a mind to waste it on teaching—no offense intended." Drew's tone was dry and brusque. "I finally relented. To make a long story short, I was president of Bradford Electronics by the age of thirty, and my father retired knowing his life's work was in good hands. He died two years later."

"Oh, Drew—I am sorry," Chelsie murmured, not knowing what else to say.

Whatever sorrow he may still have felt at the mention of his father's death was carefully camou-

flaged behind the indifference written on his face.
"That's okay," he said, his voice denying any emotion. "Anyway, over vehement protests from the
Board of Directors, I resigned last year as president to
finally try my hand at teaching. But I don't know. . . ."
A scowl creased Drew's forehead. "I made that
damned company what it is today, honey. It's my
baby and I don't know if I can give it up."

"So you stay on the Board of Directors and teach
until you can make that decision?" Chelsie prompted,
as surprised by the fact he had chosen to confide in
her as she was by the dilemma he faced.

"That's about the long and the short of it. I've
promised the Board they'll have my decision one way
or the other by Christmas." An edge underlined
Drew's voice.

Chelsie didn't know what to say to this man. The
decision would have been an easy one for her, but
then she had grown up in the academic world and it
was the only one she knew. With both her father and
mother teaching, it had been a natural choice for her.
She loved her world of books and students and was
comfortable within its secure walls. She knew next to
nothing of the business world and the desire to know
more about it was decidedly lacking in her.

Chelsie suddenly realized they had both fallen silent
and were deeply absorbed in their own thoughts. She
glanced up from her piña colada to see the swimming
pool that had brought her here in the first place. It
appeared to be straight out the sliding glass doors at
the back of the cabin, enclosed by a high, thickly
planted hedge to insure privacy. Just beyond the pool
was a small wooden structure.

"Is that a sauna?" she wondered aloud.

"Huh?" Drew Bradford came back to her with an effort, from wherever he had been.

Chelsie pointed to the structure in question. "I was just wondering if that was a sauna?" she reiterated.

"Yes, it is," he drawled, his attention fully focused on her. "Would you like to take a sauna before we go swimming?" There was the slightest flicker of something in the gray eyes, but it was gone before Chelsie could be sure.

"Hum—it does sound rather delicious, doesn't it?" she remarked after due consideration. "The thing is, I—ah didn't think to bring a swim suit. Well, why would I? I had no idea you even had a pool. Do you have an extra suit about that might fit me?" she asked stumblingly.

Drew turned and regarded her for some seconds before he answered. "You've been reading too many books about how the super rich live, my dear Chelsie. Contrary to popular belief, I do not keep an assortment of women's swimwear on hand." His laughter softened to a smile. "However, if modesty permits, may I suggest that your panties and bra probably show no more of you than a bikini would? And I can offer the added benefit of a large bath towel, if you wish." He seemed to be thoroughly enjoying the fun he was having at her expense.

"You probably don't have the sauna heated, anyway," she said evasively, looking away.

"Oh—but I do. I turned the heat on just before I left to pick you up for lunch." Drew went on, smoothly, his eyes on her, "I usually spend a few minutes in the sauna each evening before I go for a swim."

Somehow Chelsie had known he was going to say that. Well—she wasn't some young girl to be frightened off at the prospect of sharing a sauna with this man. Not if the bath towel was as large as he said.

"I accept your offer of one large bath towel, then," she replied with dignity.

Drew gulped down the remainder of his drink and briskly got to his feet. "Come along, doctor. I'll show you where you can change."

He grasped Chelsie's hand in his without giving her the opportunity to finish her own drink, and led her up the stairway to the second-story loft. They went down a hallway and came out in what had to be the master bedroom. Drew's bedroom—the thought went through her mind as she took in the king-size brass bed with an old-fashioned quilt for a cover.

"You're welcome to change in here," he said, calling her attention to the spacious bath off the bedroom. Drew dug around in the linen closet for a moment and emerged with a stack of freshly laundered towels. "Help yourself to whatever you need, honey. Perhaps you'd like to throw this on until you get down to the sauna." He held out a man's terrycloth robe for her inspection.

"Thank you." Chelsie smiled mechanically, as she took the robe from his hands.

"I'll see you downstairs in a few minutes, then," Drew stated in a no-nonsense tone. He quietly closed the door behind him as he left the room.

The young woman simply stood there after he had gone, making no move to discard her khaki blouse and gabardine pants in favor of the borrowed toweling robe. It suddenly occurred to Chelsie that she had placed herself in a most vulnerable position when it came to Drew Bradford—a position in which she may have subconsciously hoped to find herself.

There was little doubt in her mind that the physical attraction she felt for this man was unprecedented in her twenty-eight, nearly twenty-nine years. In fact, Drew Bradford was a combination of the three deadliest attributes in a man—intelligence, humor, and sensuality. It was indeed a lethal triumvirate.

But dammit, there was more to a relationship than even that! she cried out to herself. What of friendship and respect and love? Didn't these, too, have to exist between a man and a woman? They did for her, Chelsie sternly reminded herself.

Then she began to laugh—a soft little mirthless laugh in the back of her throat—as she recalled the scene between Drew and herself that very afternoon in the park. Where had all her high ideals been then? She had been swept along on a tide of passion without a thought for friendship or respect or love.

Or was love sometimes born of such a nameless passion? She knew it wasn't always a slowly emerging realization between two people, but she had always assumed somehow that it would be that way for her. She had never been one to rush in where angels fear to tread, and she was not about to start now. She was a level-headed mature woman and she would behave accordingly! With that self-admonition, Chelsie began to undress.

Still, it was with some trepidation and no small amount of self-consciousness that she made her way downstairs a few minutes later. It was all well and good for Drew to say that her bra and panties would reveal no more than a bikini, but he had not seen the skimpy, nearly see-through bits of lace she was wearing under the towel. Chelsie pulled the tie of the robe even tighter about her waist, her bare feet making soft padding sounds on the hardwood floors.

With Drew nowhere in sight, Chelsie decided the sensible thing was to go on ahead of him to the sauna. She opened the sliding glass door to the pool area and slipped through. A brief walk brought her to her destination. She opened the door to the sauna and stepped inside.

It took no more than a blink of her startled blue eyes for Chelsie to realize that Drew was already comfortably settled inside. He was sitting on a bench in the corner, as nonchalant as one could please, apparently wearing nothing more than a towel hitched about his lean hips.

His eyes flickered open, giving her a warm welcome of their own even before he spoke.

"It might be wise to hang your robe on the hook outside," he commented, without a hint of innuendo. "It gets pretty hot in here." This was added as an afterthought, somehow making his suggestion seem only a matter of common sense.

Chelsie wordlessly complied, then drew in a deep breath of courage as she settled herself on the bench next to his. The absence of small talk weighed heavily on her as she fussed and fidgeted with the towel loosely secured sarong-style about her body. Her eyes traveled reluctantly to Drew's.

"You haven't had a great deal of experience with this kind of thing, have you?" The man's voice was low. His words hovered in the hot dry air between them.

"No, I haven't," Chelsie confessed with a sigh. "I've

only been in a sauna once before." She took his question at face value and answered accordingly.

"You need to take it slow and easy then," he said, without turning his head. "Just sit back and relax, honey. That's what a sauna is supposed to do, you know—relax the mind and body."

Easy for him to say, Chelsie thought, but she was sitting there so aware of him beside her, casually attired in a flimsy towel as though it didn't bother him in the least, that relaxing was about the last thing she was capable of.

Drew stretched his long bare legs out in front of him, unconsciously drawing her attention to their tanned muscular appearance. Strong legs, legs that showed the miles he ran in their fitness, legs that could wrap themselves around hers like a vice . . . despite the heat, she shivered at the thoughts that wove back and forth through her mind like sensuous threads.

Drew moved to fold his arms across his broad chest, his skin beginning to glisten with the perspiration brought on by the intensified heat in the small room. The air was stifling, but Chelsie knew that her own intense awareness of Drew was responsible for the feeling of restriction of her breathing.

It had been a mistake to mention the sauna, she realized that now. She didn't need to sit in a small confined space with this man—both of them in a state of near nudity—to find his presence a threat, a temptation. She must have been insane to think she could handle being with him like this. Under the circumstances, it was almost more than Chelsie could take.

All the fancy words in the world couldn't help her

now. Her imagination kept taking her into those powerful arms, feeling that mouth on hers, those hands caressing her skin.

Chelsie McBride! She chastised herself. Look at the man—he isn't paying you the slightest bit of notice. Surely as a grown woman she could emulate his nonchalant attitude about the whole affair. But Chelsie had her doubts—serious doubts—that she could pull it off. What she really needed was a distraction and there was so little to distract oneself with in a sauna. She wished she had a book with her—at least that way she could pretend to read.

Then her gaze lighted on Drew's feet. That was it! She would concentrate on his feet. He had relatively nice ones as feet go, and long straight toes, but no one's feet could be thought of as sexually enticing—at least not for her.

A droll smile bowed her mouth as she examined the subject matter further. She may have inadvertently even chuckled once or twice. But at least her new occupation was temporarily keeping her out of trouble.

"I never knew anyone who found taking a sauna funny," mumbled Drew beside her, as his eyes fluttered open. "What *are* you doing?"

Chelsie gave a little shrug. "I was looking at your feet."

"My feet?" he said with a faint cynical smile.

"Under the circumstances, it seemed the safest place *to* look," she replied, a shade haughtily.

Drew's lips twitched in an effort not to smile. "For your first time you've been in here long enough, anyway."

"It's my second time," Chelsie corrected him, "but I

have had enough." She put her chin up regally and with as much grace as she could muster walked out the door. Tossing the robe over one arm, she was halfway around the pool when she heard Drew call out to her.

"Hey, where do you think you're going?" She turned to see him still standing by the sauna door, hands perched on his hips just above the towel. "You have to take a shower to stabilize your body heat," he explained, pointing to several stalls next to the sauna.

Chelsie did an about-face and retraced her steps to the sauna. "You could have told me," she sniffed, opening the shower door and stepping inside.

Drew raised his eyes upward, indicating the need for patience. "There's shampoo and soap on a shelf by your elbow if you care to use either," he said dryly.

"Thank you," Chelsie replied with a politeness that fooled neither of them.

There was something very nerve-racking about taking off all of her clothes—what few remained—knowing that Drew was in a similar state of dishabille only inches away. But Chelsie did find the invigorating shower enjoyable nonetheless. She even took advantage of the shampoo to wash her hair. Then, squeaky clean from top to bottom, she turned off the spray and reached for the toweling robe flung over the shower stall. Her underthings were still too damp to be put back on.

A moment later Drew came out of the adjoining stall, a fresh towel his only apparel. Riffling his fingers through the mat of wet hair that dripped onto his bare shoulders, he glanced up at her.

"Ready for that swim now, honey?" he asked in a cheerful voice.

"You've got to be kidding!" exclaimed Chelsie. "Thanks anyway, but I've had enough for one day," she said, with a decisive nod of her head.

"Then why don't you get us a cold drink while I do a few laps?"

"All right—" She hesitated. "What would you like?"

"Whatever you're having," he said amiably. "Just put mine on the table over there. I'll join you when I'm finished."

"Yessir, professor!" She tipped him a smart salute and turned away. Before she had gone more than a step or two, Chelsie felt the stinging snap of a towel on her backside.

"Watch your tongue, woman. You do remember what happened the last time you let it get away from you?"

With an appropriate rejoinder on the tip of that very tongue, she started to turn back to Drew. Then the realization that he had only one towel with him and that that one had been wrapped around his waist stopped her cold.

Good Lord! Was he actually standing there behind her *au naturel?* He was an *arrogant* bastard. Chelsie fervently wished she had the nerve to turn and confront Drew, but the coward in her won the day.

"I'll be sure to put plenty of ice in your drink, *darling,*" she purred sweetly, too sweetly. "It might help to cool you off." Then with a seductive swing to her hips, she sauntered toward the house.

Chelsie took her own sweet time deciding what to take from the refrigerator. Essence of hemlock was her first choice, but Drew seemed a little low on hemlock at the moment. She finally settled on a bottle of dry white wine.

When she padded back to poolside with two glasses balanced in her hands, she saw Drew still vigorously stroking up and down in the heated pool. It didn't take a vivid imagination or even very good eyesight to tell that he preferred to do his swimming in the buff. Well, she could take whatever he chose to dish out—or at least that's what she told herself.

Setting his wine on the table as he had instructed, Chelsie stretched out on one of the lounge chairs at the end of the pool. She clasped her own glass lightly between her fingers and watched the long, lithe form go through its paces.

Do what he would, she was not going to allow this man to intimidate her a moment longer. Perhaps he thought to shock or embarrass her or God knew what by strutting around in the nude like some popinjay. Well, the male form held no surprises for her. She'd grown up with a houseful of brothers. They were all pretty much the same when it got right down to the basics!

But Chelsie had to admit there was a difference this time. She wanted this man with a hunger she had felt for no other. Past passions were but feeble things compared to the uncontrollable emotions Drew Bradford seemed to arouse in her. As she watched him glide through the water, his muscles straining against his skin, she felt desire concentrate in the pit of her stomach like a time bomb about to explode.

Before she could adequately douse all evidence of that desire, he swam up to the edge of the swimming pool and stood in the waist-deep water. There was a guarded expression on his face as they both glanced simultaneously at the towel lying there just out of his reach.

"Throw me that towel, will you, Chelsie?"

"Sure," she replied airily, leaning over to pick it up. She gave it a good toss and watched as it landed within his grasp. In one easy movement Drew rose from the water and unhurriedly wrapped it about his waist. "Modest little thing, aren't you?" Chelsie muttered under her breath.

Drew looked at her in cool appraisal. "Did you say something?"

She met his gaze with a challenging tilt of her chin. "I poured you a glass of wine. I hope that's all right."

"Excellent choice," he said, taking a taste. "Sauvignon Blanc is one of my favorites, actually." As he stood there towering over her, he seemed to drink in more than just the wine. He allowed his gaze to wander lazily over her half-reclining form. "You look very enticing, my dear Chelsie, with your hair all atumble like that." Drew idly fingered the lapels of her robe, his palms brushing against her breasts in a deliberately provocative move. "And you definitely do something for terrycloth." He bent over her and ran his tongue along her lips. "Hm—you taste good, too." He returned for a second taste just to be certain, this time drinking more deeply.

Drew extracted the wineglass from Chelsie's hand without seeking or needing her approval and set it on the wrought iron patio table next to his own. Then he leisurely took the several steps that brought him back to her side. He sat down on the edge of the lounge chair and reached for her, pulling her body against his.

Chelsie wordlessly burrowed her face into his chest as her hands slipped around to his back.

His skin was still damp from his swim and slick to the touch. Chelsie inhaled the scent of him, a strange but intoxicating combination of wine and chlorine and a dusky aroma that might have been the result of his soap or shampoo. She could detect the steady rhythm of his heart giving life to every muscle and pore and gratefully pressed her lips to the spot.

Drew gently raised her head, tracing the line of her jaw with one hand, then the bare only slightly tanned throat, until he finally worked his way to the shoulder beneath her robe.

"Chelsie—" His voice was a raw whisper. "What am I going to do about wanting you?"

No answer was forthcoming. Chelsie *had* no answer for him. She could only ask herself what she was going to do about wanting him. Bemused and more than a little bewildered, she shook her head.

"I don't know either," he groaned. A muffled expletive followed as he buried his face in the mass of damp curls at her neck. He lingered there as though he were entranced with the scent of her. Then lips surprisingly warm and as smooth as satin grazed the tip of her ear and traced a sensuous path along her bare shoulder. Their light touch sent queer little shivers coursing through Chelsie.

As Drew brought his head up to seek her mouth in further sensual quest, he must have released a lever on the lounge. For as he came nearer Chelsie felt herself eased backwards until she was lying flat with him on top of her.

For a moment she thought to voice a protest at such

an obvious seduction ploy, but then Drew was distracting her with persuasive diversionary tactics and her words were all but forgotten.

It was such sweet forgetfulness to be carried along on the wings of passion with no thought for tomorrow or yesterday or even the next minute. Everything was here and now as their mouths moved and tongues probed and teeth nibbled at the urging of their rising passion.

Drew's mouth was seductive, persuasive. His breath came hot and fast as he sought to awaken in her the same driving need he felt in himself.

"Damn, honey—I did try to keep away from you!" he swore, as he tore his mouth reluctantly from hers. "I even swam double the number of laps I usually do. I had some foolish idea it might cool my ardor. But I want you more than ever."

Chelsie's heart slammed against her chest. "And I want you, Drew," she said in a low, earnest voice.

He stretched out to cover her completely so that their bodies fit together like two missing pieces of the same puzzle. The hard pressure of his pelvis bore down into her hip bones, turning them to liquid fire. With his tongue he drew a line from the slight indentation in her chin to the shadowy hollow between her breasts.

With all their moving about the terry robe had begun to work itself free from Chelsie's body. Very soon she feared the only barrier separating them would be the towel about Drew's hips.

The thought of making love—*really* making love— with this man sent an arrow of piercing need down her frame to the aching emptiness below. She twisted and turned beneath him, not in any effort to escape or thwart his explorations, but simply because Chelsie could not bear to lie there stone still.

Then Drew retreated an inch or two and watched the play of emotions on her languid features. Chelsie opened her eyes and found that his had become a deep velvety shade of green such as she had never seen before. Never taking his eyes from hers, he untied the robe and eased it away from her body.

"You're beautiful," he murmured, as his hands came up to see for themselves. "Your body is as exciting as your mind. It makes a man want to bury himself in your softness."

He lightly ran his fingers down her breasts in a feathery caress, then watched, intrigued, as each nipple curled up into a hard point of arousal. The action brought a throaty groan from her as if she were in some kind of exquisite pain. She instinctively clasped his head between her hands and brought his mouth down to her. As she arched her back in an unconsciously erotic move, her flesh was sent deep into his mouth.

He caressed and manipulated each ripe bud with the full power of his considerable expertise, until Chelsie thought she could stand no more. He caught the hardened nipple between his teeth and bit down just enough to elicit a response from her. Then his mouth blazed a trail down one breast, across her abdomen, and back up the other side, until both pink tips stood at attention.

Drew let his eyes feast upon the golden body lying half beneath his. He ran his hand down her from shoulder to thigh with nothing to stop him. Chelsie reached out to stroke the hard, flat plane of his stomach, her caress bringing forth an answering moan of pleasure from him. Made bold by his response to her touch, she drew an imaginary line with her fingernail from the mat of dark hair on his chest to the few small curls at his navel.

"Oh, God, Chelsie—I—" But the words would not come. Perhaps the magic between them was too new and too fragile to be labeled with standard phrases. Phrases that so often were no more than empty, meaningless syllables.

"I know. . . ." she whispered, putting her hand to his mouth.

Then—whether by accident or design—the towel about Drew's hips worked free and slipped to the ground. Now when they came together there was not the slightest barrier to their pleasure. They touched and caressed and explored, knowing in their hearts where their mutual passion must lead them.

Chelsie had never felt like this before. When Drew kissed her it was as though he were making love to her—mind, body, and soul.

"Drew—" She tried to tell him of the strange ache inside her that only he could assuage.

"Chelsie, honey—I need you," he said in his softest tone.

He pulled back for a moment and read the need reflected in her eyes. Then his hand slid down her body to part her thighs. His body sought hers with a need that could be no longer denied. Chelsie wrapped herself around him and rose up in body and spirit to join him on that ultimate quest for ecstasy. They followed the road together and when the end was in view, they cried out their mutual joy and fulfillment.

Chelsie lay there in the circle of Drew's arms, his body still covering hers. She wondered at the strange and glorious feeling that had entered her heart and mind at the moment of truth. Here was a man who could make love a wondrous thing, and for that she loved him. Sex was not everything in a relationship, not for a woman like Chelsie. But a healthy physical attraction between a man and a woman was the cornerstone to any enduring relationship.

She nuzzled the baby-soft spot by his ear and gently blew at a wisp of hair that had strayed across it. Drew slowly raised his head from her shoulder and stared at her with a depth of emotion that stunned Chelsie.

"Something special . . . something really rare has happened between us, Chelsie," he admitted in a strained voice. "And it's something I can't wait to repeat," he growled, as he nuzzled her neck in turn.

"Drew—" she chuckled, a small, cozy sound. "Behave yourself!"

A faint amusement crossed his face. "Too late for that now, doctor. I've allowed myself to be corrupted by a pretty young thing with big blue eyes and sun-streaked hair. No doubt she'll be the ruin of me yet," he mused, absently combing his fingers through her hair.

"You'll just have to learn to take your medicine like everybody else," she teased, giving him a light tap on the tip of his nose.

Drew cupped her chin in his hand too firmly for it to be a caress. "I hope you understand that you're all mine now, babe," he said in a quiet voice. The expression he turned to her bore no trace of compromise.

"Now wait just a minute, Drew Bradford—"

He interrupted her with an exasperated snort. "Tut, tut, *darling*—remember that tongue of yours."

Then they laughed together, where only moments before they had been in a state of mutual euphoria. Drew slowly got to his feet and held out his hand to her. She took it without hesitation. He led her into the house and up the stairs and this time when they showered they did so together and without a shred of self-consciousness.

Drew soaped her back and Chelsie lathered his chest and they laughed and kissed and afterward made love a second time on the big brass bed.

5

For what seemed like the tenth time in an hour, Chelsie McBride threw her pen down on the desk and went along to the kitchen to make herself a cup of coffee.

She stood staring out the small window above the kitchen sink, hands posed on jean-clad hips, while the automatic coffeemaker hummed and hawed and finally produced a fresh pot of coffee. She poured a cup, added milk and sugar, and returned to the big desk in the living room where a stack of papers were awaiting her attention.

For the past several years, Chelsie had spent more Friday nights than she cared to count doing just what she was doing tonight, reviewing students' essays and planning her classes for the coming week. It was entirely beside the point that she had mounds of neglected paperwork to catch up on, thanks to Andrew Bradford.

Drew! She felt a warm surge of color rush to her face at the thought of him. Drew—bright red spots in the center of her cheeks faded to pink as, for the hundredth time, he occupied her mind to the exclusion of all else. What on this God's earth was she to do about Drew?

After that wondrous afternoon of lovemaking, she had seen him every day this week. But with one major difference—there had been no more such moments of intimacy between them.

Drew had taken her out to dinner on Tuesday evening to a local restaurant that was low on atmosphere but served excellent food. On Wednesday they had gone to a movie—a comedy whose name she had already forgotten, if indeed she had ever known it. And just the night before he had escorted her to a cello recital at the college.

He had made even more plans for them to spend the weekend together and then that very afternoon had stopped by her office between classes to inform her that he had been called away on urgent business: Business that could not be postponed, that would take the entire weekend.

Chelsie had tried to smile and reassure him that she understood, but feelings of disappointment and hurt and even anger had gone through her as he spoke. With one hard, swift kiss, Drew had bid her an abrupt goodbye and left her standing there to deal with her disappointment—and a now long, empty weekend— on her own.

It had only added fuel to the fire of growing doubts she was having about her budding relationship with the man. He had been subtle about it, but there was no mistaking the fact that he was deliberately avoiding any kind of sexual contact with her. Since that Monday, Drew had made very sure they did not find themselves alone or in circumstances that could be a prelude to intimacy.

It was only natural then that Chelsie should begin to ask herself why. Perhaps he regretted getting involved with her in the first place. What if their dates this past week had been no more than Drew's way of letting her down easy? The thought sent a surprisingly sharp pain through her. She prayed it was not so, but she didn't know what else to make of his cavalier behavior.

On each of the last three nights, Drew had picked her up at Esther Freeman's and politely returned her there several hours later. He never once mentioned coming up for a cup of coffee, nor had he issued any invitation for Chelsie to visit his home—where they might at least have been afforded some privacy.

She was mystified by his actions, yet she knew there had been something special between them that afternoon. Drew had said as much himself. Surely his words had been more than just the idle pillow talk of a man on the make. Chelsie could not allow herself to think that for her own peace of mind—but then peace of mind was not always so easily come by.

As hard as she might try, she could come up with no other possible explanation. She didn't know what to make of the man she had somehow gotten herself involved with. And now the whole long weekend stretched out in front of her like some desolate landscape with no relief in view.

Chelsie took a sip from the cup in her hand and

realized she had once more let it get cold on her. She dumped the coffee back in the pot and poured herself another cup.

Perhaps it was just as well Drew had gone away for the weekend. She had some serious thinking to do—and somehow when she was with him all semblance of reason flew out of her mind.

She suspected the intense feelings she had for Drew sprang from their physical attraction to each other. How could she deny even to herself that his lovemaking had opened a new door in her life? She knew if she were wise she would guard her heart carefully, but the heart so often did not care what was wise.

It was as if a raging tempest had blown into her life, rearranged everything, and then just as quickly blown away again. Chelsie hated the thought that she might have been an easy mark for him almost as much as the possibility that he might be the kind of man looking for one. There was no kidding herself on that score—women were drawn to Drew Bradford like bees to honey. She was certain he had had his share and no doubt turned down many more. It was of little comfort to know she had at least not been one of the latter.

Chelsie McBride was not the kind of woman to engage in a casual affair. The thought that she may have done just that in a moment of passion was abhorrent to her. It lessened the respect she had always had for herself as a strongminded, independent woman who *thought* first and *felt* second.

This was getting her nowhere, she thought, rubbing the sore spot on her temple that signaled a headache was coming on. Then she realized she was hungry and that was doubtless the reason her head had begun to ache.

Chelsie opened the cupboard and rummaged around until she found a box of tea biscuits, and then, coffee and snack in hand, she forced herself to face the stack of papers on her desk. She had never allowed her personal life to interfere with her professional responsibilities and she wasn't going to start now. She took the job of teaching seriously, almost with religious dedication. Consequently, Dr. Chelsie McBride was regarded with undisputed respect by both faculty and students alike.

She picked up a short essay comparing Chaucer's first three tales—the tenth she had looked at that evening—and began to read. But her mind refused to cooperate. She had Drew Bradford on the brain and it seemed he would stay there in spite of what she might do.

Chelsie found herself recalling in intimate detail the feel of his hard male form pressed against her, the strong powerful hands that played her body like a master musician touching all the right chords, the lips that set her ablaze, turning her into a creature of mindless passion. She relived the moment of possession and the explosion of pure sensual delight that followed.

Good Lord! She would never get through the pile of essays at this rate. Why did she allow Drew Bradford to distract her so when he wasn't even there in the flesh?

The question remained unanswered as a soft knock came at Chelsie's apartment door. Just for a moment she thought . . . she hoped it might be Drew. Silly of her. Drew was in Albany, nearly a hundred miles away, and wouldn't be returning until his first class on Monday.

Still, some small spark of hope refused to die, and when Chelsie opened the door and saw it was Lynn Marshall, disappointment must have shown itself on her face.

"Hi, Lynn!" She tried to instill enthusiasm into her voice, to somehow make up for the disappointment she had allowed the other woman to see.

"For your sake, I wish I were about six feet tall with dark hair and gray eyes—but I'm afraid it's only me," Lynn said apologetically.

Chelsie duly chastised herself. "I'm sorry, Lynn. It's just that—"

"There's no need to explain," the brunette cut in adroitly. "I understand. Believe me—I do. I am kind of surprised to find you at home, though."

Chelsie spread out her hands in a gesture of resignation. "Drew had to go away on business this weekend. So I'm doing some much needed paperwork. Do you have time to come in or are you on your way out somewhere?"

"Frank and I are going to a movie, but he won't be here for another quarter of an hour," Lynn replied, stepping inside and finding a chair on her own. "How have you been?" she asked with a guarded expression.

"I've been fine." Chelsie realized that the other woman had wanted to ask much more and hadn't, out of respect for her privacy.

"Are your classes going well?" A perfectly reasonable question, but one she hazarded Lynn had posed strictly to keep them off the subject of Professor Andrew Bradford.

"My classes are going great. They're a little larger than I'd been promised originally, but that always seems to be the case. How are the French lessons progressing?"

"*Entendu!*" Lynn grinned. "Chelsie, I know it's none of my business, but you aren't getting involved with Andrew Bradford, are you?" The words came fast and furious out of Lynn's mouth, as though they had done so without her permission.

"Is there some reason why I shouldn't go out with him?" Chelsie asked defensively.

"Oh—now I've gone and done it!" groaned the brunette. "I've stuck my big nose in where it doesn't belong, as if you were a kid and me the mother hen." Lynn Marshall appeared genuinely contrite, but she continued nonetheless. "You happen to be a very sweet person. I don't mean that to sound insipid— you're just one heck of a nice woman, and there's nothing you can do to change that."

"Well, thank you, Lynn," Chelsie swallowed a condescending smile, "but what in the world does all of that have to do with Drew Bradford?"

Lynn Marshall was unable to meet that steady blue gaze with one of her own. "You seem different the past few days," she mumbled. Then the woman brought her head up. Concerned eyes looked out at Chelsie. "I know you've been going out with Drew Bradford all this week. I saw the two of you at the concert last night. And each time I see you with him, you seem sad somehow. Oh, I don't know, Chelsie—" Her hands expressed her confusion. "I guess I just hate to think the man might do something to hurt you. You're too nice for any man to do that to you."

"Lynn—Drew and I really don't know each other very well." At least that was no fabrication. Chelsie made a gesture with her hands if she were searching for the right words. "We enjoy each other's company, and he's asked me to go out with him a couple of times." She felt her face fall an inch or two. "I—I don't know how I feel about him, Lynn." Her voice was so low it was scarcely audible to the woman who sat only a foot or two from her. "Drew is different from the men I usually meet. He's really very good company, you know." But her vulnerability shone through loud and clear.

"Oh, God, Chelsie—you aren't falling for him?" There was little doubt that that spelled doomsday in Lynn Marshall's book.

What could she say? That was the very question Chelsie had carefully avoided asking herself all week. Afraid of what her heart might tell her, she had purposely steered clear of analyzing her feelings.

Chelsie closed her eyes and shuddered. "I honestly don't know, Lynn," she finally answered, a kind of desperation in her voice.

"Listen—I didn't come over here to give you the third degree like some kind of self-appointed surrogate mother," Lynn said, with a gentleness that touched the other woman's heart. "Actually, I came by to see if you would like to go out with Frank and Gerry and me on Sunday afternoon. Frank has four tickets for an all-star baseball game up at Cooperstown."

Chelsie made an expressive grimace. "I don't care much for baseball."

"Don't tell Frank—but it bores me to tears!" confessed Lynn, with a conspiratorial grin. "I promise you the four of us will have fun together, and Gerry has been dying to see you again." Lynn tried every method of persuasion she could think of. "It's better than sitting around this apartment all day by yourself. I'll treat you to as many hot dogs as you can eat—"

Whether it was on that last count or not, she was never to know, but Lynn Marshall was duly rewarded for her efforts as Chelsie finally nodded her agreement.

"All right—I give up! I'll go," she laughed. "You should be in sales, Lynn. You're wasted teaching French."

"*C'est vrai,*" sighed the woman with a typically Frenchwomanlike shrug. "Say— why don't you come to the movie with Frank and me tonight? It's supposed to be a very funny comedy, and frankly, you look like you could use a few laughs."

"That's sweet of you to ask, but I've seen it. Besides, I have got to finish these essays if it's the last thing I do," Chelsie replied in a brisk tone.

"You're so dedicated. I'd probably feel guilty if I let myself," Lynn said with a wry smile. "Well, I think that's Frank's size twelve feet I hear coming up the stairs now, so I'd better dash. I'll drop by tomorrow and let you know what time on Sunday."

"Thanks Lynn—for everything!" Chelsie called after her.

The brunette stopped when she reached the door and turned back for a moment. "Hey—you never told me if the movie was any good."

Chelsie responded with a rollicking laugh. "I don't recall the first thing about it, including the title."

"Gee, that good, huh?"

"I promise you'll never notice the difference with Frank at your side," she teased.

Lynn looked thoughtful for a moment and then returned her smile with a wink. "That's true!"

Then she was out the door and down the hall.
Chelsie could hear her greeting Frank Dixon as he
trudged up the last few steps. Then Lynn dropped her
voice, but it carried to Chelsie's door nonetheless:

"Hey, Frank—can you get us four tickets for Sunday's Basball Hall of Fame game?"

With a broad smile on her face, Chelsie McBride
closed her apartment door and went back to work.

Chelsie had known women who met up with an old
high school flame at the ten-year class reunion and
discovered much to their surprise and dream-
shattering dismay that Prince Charming now had a
protruding waistline, a receding hairline, and had
somehow grown incredibly dull in the intervening
years. After twelve years, she was quite otherwise
surprised when she saw Gerry Marshall again for the
first time.

He still had the blondest hair she had ever seen on a
man and the bluest eyes, but the years had been good
to Gerry, at least on the surface. He was even better
looking at twenty-nine than he had been during their
high school days. The big difference, she quickly
discovered, was in his personality. His teenage cocki-
ness had been replaced by a certain hesitancy, at least
with Chelsie, that was rather charming. It took no
more than a few minutes on her part, however, to
realize that the old "zing" between them had mellowed into nothing more than friendship.

Lynn was right. The four of them did have a good
time together. After a few awkward moments at the
beginning, they found themselves laughing and remi-
niscing the way old friends should.

And the baseball game wasn't nearly as boring as

she had feared. In fact, it had turned out to be quite funny at times, much to the chagrin of the two teams playing that afternoon. She and Lynn had even managed to appear halfway interested when Frank and Gerry insisted that no trip to Cooperstown was complete without a tour of the National Baseball Hall of Fame and Museum.

Chelsie's personal preference would have been a tour of Fenimore House, home of James Fenimore Cooper, who had described this region of New York in his *Leatherstocking Tales,* but it was already late afternoon when the four of them piled back into Frank Dixon's car and headed home.

All in all it had been an enjoyable Sunday and Chelsie said as much to her three companions as they walked in the front door at Esther Freeman's.

"Would you like to come to my place for a cup of coffee?" she offered, as they rather noisily climbed the stairway to the second floor.

"I think we'll take a raincheck," smiled Lynn, a meaningful look passing between her and Frank Dixon. "Frank has promised to show me a few of the defensive moves he learned as a linebacker."

With a sheepish grin on his face, the big man shrugged his shoulders. "Well, it sure beats 'let me show you my etchings.'"

"I'd love a cup of coffee, if the offer is still good," Gerry Marshall put in.

Chelsie turned to him with laughter still fresh on her face. "Sure—c'mon, Ger—maybe we can come up with a few defensive moves of our own."

He gave her a wolfish grin for Lynn and Frank's benefit. "Now that's an offer I can't refuse!"

"Do you remember Angela Martin?" giggled Chelsie, as she and Gerry continued on down the hall to her apartment. "I wonder what ever happened to her."

"I ran into Angela not long ago. All of her taste is still in her mouth," he managed with a straight face.

"Oh, Gerry—you're incorrigible! You haven't really changed at all under that crusty newspaperman exterior," she laughed, taking out her keys and unlocking the door.

The moment Chelsie McBride walked into her apartment she sensed that something was different. It was an instantaneous impression that coincided with the sight of Andrew Bradford comfortably sprawled in one of her living room chairs.

She had read, of course, of awkward moments like this—when the heroine brings one man home only to find another waiting for her, but she had assumed it happened only in novels. Unlike the undaunted heroines of fiction, she had no clever retort on the tip of her tongue with which to handle the situation.

Drew was the first to speak. "Hello, Chelsie," he said, not moving.

She fixed him with large, reproachful blue eyes. "I—I thought you said you wouldn't be back until tomorrow," she stammered, knowing she sounded guilty, *looked* guilty of God knew what—and that made her all the angrier. What in the hell was Drew doing here in her apartment, anyway? That's what she really wanted to ask, to demand of him.

"I managed to clear up the problem in Albany sooner than I expected," he replied offhandedly, as he flicked at an imaginary speck of lint on his dark suit. But he didn't fool Chelsie. She had seen the look in his eyes.

"You should have called first," she snapped rather peevishly. "Why else do you think God invented telephones?"

"God didn't—it was Alexander Graham Bell. And I did call, but since you weren't home you obviously couldn't know that," Drew replied, his voice quiet, dangerously quiet.

It was finally left to an unsuspecting Gerry Marshall to break the tension that filled the room. As if on cue, he cleared his throat to alert the couple's attention to his presence.

Chelsie turned to him with an apologetic smile on her face, "Oh, Gerry—I'm sorry. Please come in," she urged, taking his arm and drawing him further into the apartment. "This is Andrew Bradford, a fellow faculty member at the State College," she began, deliberately relegating Drew to the rank of professional acquaintance. She knew that would irk him, and it did. She saw the slight narrowing of his eyes with a smug feeling of satisfaction. Drew unfolded his legs and rose from the chair as she continued. "This is an old friend of mine, Gerry Marshall."

"An old boyfriend, actually," grinned the younger man, as he accepted the handshake Drew extended.

Knowing she might well have to pay for it later, Chelsie seized the opportunity unwittingly provided by Gerry Marshall and played it to the hilt. In her opinion, a touch of the old "green-eyed monster" would considerably improve the personality of one Professor Andrew Bradford.

"Yes, Gerry and I were high school sweethearts," Chelsie murmured in a low sultry voice, laying it on as thick as she dared.

"High school sweethearts. . . ." drawled the older

man in a dry voice, his gray eyes flicking briefly over the couple. "Well, I hate to break up your little reunion, but Chelsie and I have some unfinished business to attend to," he stated rather pointedly.

The woman felt her face darken with anger. She vowed she would get him for this one day.

"Gerry and I were about to have some coffee, Drew. I'm sure our business can wait," she said, determined to assert herself.

His eyebrows rose fractionally. "Oh, but, I'm afraid it can't," insisted Drew, the mocking look back in his eyes.

"Listen, Chelsie—" Gerry Marshall stepped forward. "It's time I was going, anyway. I'll take a raincheck on that coffee."

She started to protest and then thought better of it. Drew was determined to be difficult, she could see that, and the situation was by no means going to improve if Gerry stayed.

"All right, Ger," she finally agreed in a tight voice. "Thank you for this afternoon. I really did enjoy myself."

"So did I. I'll give you a call," he added, as they reached the apartment door.

"I'd like that," Chelsie said, with a reassuring smile. "I'm sorry about the coffee."

"That's okay—we'll do it next time. It really was good seeing you again, Chelsie." Then the tall blond man bent his head and kissed her lightly on the lips. "So long, old friend of mine."

The minute Gerry Marshall was out the door of her apartment and safely on his way down the stairs, Chelsie swung around to face Andrew Bradford. She suddenly wished she smoked. She could use a cigarette about now to calm her frayed nerves. It would also give her something to do with her hands—hands that were sorely tempted at the moment to strangle Drew Bradford's lousy neck!

"Well, I hope you're satisfied, professor!" she spit at him venomously, her indignation having become a very real thing. "You have just managed to drive away an old and dear friend of mine."

Drew stood there looking at her, apparently unconcerned. "Oh, is that what he was. . . ." He shook his head. "With all the references to 'old boyfriends' and 'high school sweethearts' floating around, I wasn't sure."

Chelsie straightened her back. "Gerry Marshall and I have been friends for a long time and I would like to keep it that way—which may be difficult in light of your incredible rudeness just now."

"You don't need any 'old and dear' friends like Marshall," Drew drawled in a lazy, caressing tone. "I'm the only friend you need," he said, in a low mocking voice, coming toward her with a predatory air.

"Then it's pretty obvious my idea of friendship isn't anything like yours," Chelsie said adamantly, the angry words sputtering forth from her mouth. "No one has the right to choose my friends for me—least of all you, Drew Bradford!"

"Ah, c'mon, honey, who do you think you're kidding?" He expelled a breath of indulgent laughter —laughter that did not quite reach the watchful gray eyes. "That's not the issue here, and you damn well know it! You were deliberately throwing that young pup up in my face with that high school sweethearts routine. Do you think I'm blind? I could see what you were trying to do." Drew was standing directly in front of her now bold as brass. "You were using the guy to get back at me."

Chelsie gave a light little self-conscious laugh that didn't come off as nonchalantly as she had hoped. "What could I possibly want to get back at you for?" she scoffed, as though the notion were utterly ridiculous.

"For not making love to you all week. . . ." drawled the man, as one hand came up to caress her neck.

She tried to swat at his hand, as one might an annoying insect. "You overestimate yourself, professor," she gritted through her teeth. "I'm mad because you practically threw a friend of mine out of this apartment. It has nothing to do with your so-called sexual prowess."

"That *is* it!" A light went on in his eyes. "You really are mad about the fact that I deliberately kept my distance from you this week. You were trying to make me jealous," he stated arrogantly.

Chelsie felt the heat of anger rise to her face. "I had no such juvenile thought in mind," she brusquely denied.

Drew ignored the denial as he ran his fingers through the length of silky hair that brushed her shoulders. "Well—if that was your intent, babe, then I want you to know you succeeded. I saw red when you walked in that door with young Adonis at your heels. I told you before, Chelsie—you're all mine now. I don't expect to work my tail off to get back to you a day early and find that some pretty boy from your past has stepped in as a temporary replacement while I'm away."

Drew swooped down and reestablished his claim

with lips that would brook no argument. Then he kissed her a second time, his mouth hard and unyielding, as if he wanted to make sure she was well and truly branded with his mark.

But Chelsie would not bend before the onslaught on his bruising lips and hands. Force had always appalled her, and it acquired no more attractive qualities simply because it was coming from Drew.

"Take your hands off me," she said in a voice that carried a message he clearly understood. "One afternoon of sex does not entitle you to act the part of the outraged lover." The fact that that was exactly what she had wanted to arouse in him was neatly shoved to the back of Chelsie's mind. "I am my own woman and no one is going to stake me out as his territory. I belong to no man."

"Like hell!" Drew stated autocratically. "We had more than a few hours of sex together and you know it, lady. Are you trying to tell me now that what happened between us *wasn't* special? That you do that kind of thing all the time?" Drew demanded rather nastily.

A cold pain lodged in her chest, like a dagger of ice. "No—I'm not saying that. What happened between us *was* special. But I won't have you rushing into my life like a bull in a china shop, indiscriminately breaking everything in sight."

He wiped away this consideration with a wave of his hand. "You seem a little confused, honey. You're the one who brought out the matches and lit the fire by bringing that Marshall kid here and parading him around under my nose. You should know better than to play with fire if you can't take the heat."

"You were insufferably rude," she reminded him with prim anger.

"Maybe so—but dammit, Chelsie, I've kept my hands off you for the past five days, and that was no easy task. How do you think I felt when you came in with some guy practically falling all over you?" he said, suddenly rough and surly.

"Practically falling all over me!" she hooted. "Gerry Marshall was holding my hand." Good Lord—she had tapped a well of jealousy in the man that was beyond her wildest imaginings. She must find a way to repair some of the damage she had wrought. "Look Drew—until today, Gerry and I hadn't seen each other in nearly twelve years. We really are just friends." Chelsie moistened her bottom lip. "So, maybe I did play up the old-boyfriend bit a little. But you've seemed different this week and I didn't know what to think."

A glint of satisfaction showed itself in Drew Bradford's eyes. "So—you admit you used the guy to make me jealous," he stated, obviously wanting nothing less than a full confession from her.

Chelsie threw up her hands in an exaggerated gesture. "All right—I did use Gerry. Now are you satisfied?"

"Not entirely," he said, pausing significantly. "Where were you today?" Drew demanded, assuming the role of inquisitor.

"Oh—now wait a minute. . . ." She jerked her attention up to his face. She saw something there that both gladdened her heart and frightened her just a little. But wasn't this what she had wanted? To know that Drew cared for her in some way? "You're going to feel awfully silly when I tell you," she warned him.

He watched her with an unwavering gaze. "Why don't you let me be the judge of that?"

Chelsie faced him squarely. "We went to the baseball game in Cooperstown."

"You want me to believe that after twelve years, you and what's-his-face went to a baseball game?" Drew asked, lifting one skeptical eyebrow.

"We went with Lynn Marshall, who happens to be Gerry's sister, as well as my next-door neighbor, and her date, Frank Dixon," Chelsie said, with growing irritation. "I can give you their addresses and telephone numbers—or perhaps a signed affidavit will do."

Drew gave a half-laugh and shook his head. "The guy's an even bigger fool than I gave him credit for."

"Gerry Marshall happens to be a friend and a gentleman. *He* wouldn't dream of taking advantage of a woman!" she exclaimed hotly, coming to the man's defense.

Drew gave her that appraising narrow stare again. "Are you implying, my sharp-tongued little witch, that I have somehow somewhere taken advantage of you, as you so quaintly put it?"

Chelsie shook off his hand angrily. "I didn't like your implication about Gerry—that's all," she muttered, managing to avoid a direct answer to his question.

Drew was not about to let it go that easily. "You didn't answer me, honey." His voice was threat enough, but then he began to massage the tense cord at the back of her neck in slow, sensuous circles. "Have I ever taken advantage of you, Chelsie? Forced you against your will?"

"No—" she groaned at last, feeling her traitorous body react to his touch by moving against him, much as a purring cat will rub itself against its owner.

"Do you have any idea how hard it is for me to keep you at arm's length?" He varied the question as his hands moved down to her shoulders.

Her eyes growing darker with each caress, Chelsie's lips parted involuntarily. "No—"

A scowl creased his forehead. "Well, let me tell you, sweetheart, it takes every crumb of nobility I can scrape together."

"Nobility?" Chelsie laughed, picking up on the word.

"Chelsie—it would be so easy to take you to bed again." Drew stopped her protest with one finger to her softened lips. "I want you so bad it hurts, and you want me, too, if you're honest with yourself. But I want each of us to have the chance to get to know the other better without clouding the issue with sex."

"So while we see if we *like* each other, we abstain?" she said brazenly.

Drew grasped her by the upper arms, his hands brushing against her breasts. "You tempt me, woman," he growled. "I have half a mind to forget the whole damned silly idea. But we are going to be either a one-night stand or a whole hell of a lot more. And until we decide which—yes, we abstain!"

Chelsie wiped the smirk off her face as she realized Drew meant every word he said. "And how do we decide?" she heard herself ask in a small, hesitant voice.

"To begin with, I want you to come home to Albany with me next weekend. I want you to see the other half of my world—the world of Bradford Electronics," he said in a deceptively mild tone.

"Why?" Chelsie asked, with more than a suspicion of tears in her voice.

Drew's gaze brushed her face like a touch of need. "I need to know if there is any future for us, Chelsie. Somehow in a matter of just a few days you've burrowed your way under my skin. If I make love to you again, I may not be able to let you go, honey. Do you understand?"

She found his inquiry unexpectedly difficult to answer. "I don't know, Drew," she replied truthfully.

"Will you come with me next weekend?" he repeated in the form of a question.

Chelsie McBride looked up at him and realized that she needed some answers of her own. Perhaps Drew was right. It would give them the opportunity to find out if what they felt for each other was merely infatuation or something a great deal more.

"All right—I'll come," she finally said, in measured accents.

Drew brought her into his arms then, wrapping himself around her like a mantle of warmth. His lips found hers with a tenderness that brought the tears to Chelsie's eyes. Then his mouth exploded into action as he once more sought the passion they could ignite in each other with a touch. She opened her mouth to his sensuous inquiry and answered it with one of her own. Crushed to his hard masculine form, Chelsie felt the familiar languor steal over her, turning her bones to liquid fire. She ran her fingers down the front of his shirt and entwined them about his waist, consciously pressing herself against the length of him.

"Oh, God—I must be crazy!" he groaned, as he inhaled the sweet temptation of her, his hands seeking the soft swell of her breasts. Then, with a shudder, he halted his explorations and leaned his forehead against hers. "I want you, Chelsie. You have ample proof of that. But I won't take you—not here, not now." His words were uttered with a ferocity that startled her.

"Drew—" All the desire and frustration and need she felt was expressed in that one word.

"I know—it's hard for me, too," he said gently, putting her away from him. "Trust me, honey. We've got to see this through to the end."

Chelsie could only nod her head. After all, what other choice did she have? And when Drew kissed her good night several minutes later and reluctantly left her at the door, she let him go without a word.

But the tears came hard and fast that night. Chelsie's pillow was damp with them when she finally drifted into a restless sleep where visions of a dark-haired man came to disturb her once again.

6

The following Friday was the epitome of the perfect autumn day, with its dazzling sunlight filtering down through golden trees, setting the entire scene afire with color. There was an unmistakable aroma of smoke and dried leaves in the air and a briskness that foretold the official demise of summer. It was a day when it felt good simply to be young and alive.

After their last midafternoon classes, Chelsie had assumed they would head directly along the main highway leading to the state capital. She was surprised, therefore, when Drew turned off at a side road and pulled up at the tiny Oneonta airport.

"Are we flying to Albany?" she asked incredulously, studying the rows of brightly colored airplanes that looked more like toys than the real thing.

"Yes, I keep a plane here. It saves valuable time when I need to get back and forth in a hurry," Drew explained, as he parked the station wagon beside a small building.

Chelsie's second surprise was even greater when it came. After loading their luggage in the back of the aircraft, Drew installed himself in the pilot's seat.

"Are you planning to fly this thing yourself?" she asked, giving the twin-engined Aerostar a dubious look.

"I always fly myself if I can—that way when I'm ready to go I don't have to wait around for a pilot," he explained as he began to click switches on and off and go through the necessary checklist. "Don't look so concerned, honey. I'm a duly licensed pilot with a lot of hours in the air," he reassured her before takeoff.

Chelsie sat back in the seat next to Drew, silent, knowing that her chatter would only distract him at a time when he would least appreciate it. At the moment of takeoff, she squeezed her eyes tightly shut and mumbled a quick prayer. Somehow she felt much more vulnerable in the small craft than she did on the giant commercial airplanes on which she occasionally traveled. Then she opened her eyes and began to relax, enjoying the view of blue skies above and green and brown earth below.

There was little conversation exchanged between them on the short flight. The level of noise inside the cockpit was an effective deterrent to small talk. For most of the flight, Chelsie simply gazed out the window. From their altitude of 4,400 feet, there was a great deal she could see. And she had to admit it was an unprecedented way to view the beauty of the rolling hills and mountains that surrounded Oneonta.

Hoping she had made the right choices, she let her mind wander to the clothes she had brought along for this weekend. Drew had told her there would be several parties to attend, and he'd intimated the affairs would be relatively formal. He intended taking her on a tour of Bradford Electronics, as well. Chelsie had packed her two chicest evening dresses and several smart wool suits of her own fashioning. She knew they all flattered her, but something made her wonder just the same if her homemade outfits wouldn't look out of place among the designer labels the other women were bound to be sporting.

For the first time in years, more years than she could recall, Chelsie McBride was actually afraid. She rued the day she had agreed to this experimental trip with Drew. It was the unknown factors that bothered her, and she was just beginning to realize how many unknowns there were. At least in Oneonta she felt herself on an equal footing with this man. Now—in enemy territory, she found her confidence sadly lacking.

She wasn't accustomed to private planes and fancy cars and all the other trappings of the rich. Her family had never had much money left over at the end of the month when she was growing up. With six mouths to feed and four students to eventually put through college, things had always been a little tight around the McBride household. The idea that education made a man "rich" was what her family believed.

Chelsie supposed the feeling of somehow being on social probation this weekend added to her discomfiture, but she had never thought of herself as a coward. Drew could talk all he wanted about showing her his world; she knew he was also going to judge how well she fit into that world. The only thing that kept Chelsie from being totally intimidated was the fact that she wouldn't be meeting his family—on this trip. Drew's mother was on a cruise somewhere in the Caribbean —bless her little heart!

Well—was she going to allow a few furs and gaudy diamonds to make her feel less a woman? Chelsie thought, trying to boost her spirits. With a perfunctory nod of her head, she told herself, "not by a long shot!" She was intelligent, articulate, and fairly attractive. She could meet the President himself without apology.

Then, before she knew it, Drew was back on the radio with the control tower and they were making their descent into Albany. It was apparently a familiar pattern of events for him as he easily landed the Aerostar and taxied to a small hangar at one end of the field.

They exited the airplane with their luggage and entered the office adjoining the hangar. Drew picked up a set of car keys after a few words with the man behind the desk as to their projected departure time on Sunday, and then they were once more out into the afternoon sun.

"Did you enjoy the flight?" Drew inquired, indicating the direction they were to take once they reached the parking lot.

"Yes—once we got off the ground," grinned Chelsie. "It was a beautiful day to fly. You're a very good pilot. How long have you had your license?"

"That depends on what kind you mean. I first soloed in a Piper Cub when I was sixteen."

"Sixteen!" The idea astounded her. "You were soloing in an airplane while I was managing rather thoroughly and completely to fail my first driver's test," she groaned.

"I've never known anyone who had a problem getting their driver's license," commented the man. "What happened?"

"Well—I wasn't doing too badly until I backed into a tree. . . ." Chelsie confessed sheepishly.

Drew put his head back and let out with a whooping laugh. "I should have guessed after the way we first met," he teased, his eyes shimmering with humor. He had stopped by a sleek silver automobile.

"Is this yours?" she asked, gaping at the Mercedes sedan.

"Yes—do you like it?"

"Cars are a convenient way to get from one place to another," she said, with a shrug.

"In that case, I'll drive if you don't mind," he said, and laughed heartily.

Chelsie accepted Drew's offer and settled herself in the passenger seat of the luxurious car. The drive to Albany passed quickly and comfortably, with Drew keeping up a running commentary on local points of interest and anecdotes of his years in the city. He could be excellent company when he chose to be and Chelsie soon found herself relaxing and even joining in every now and then with a story of her own. They were laughing over an incident from Chelsie's days at Bryn Mawr when Drew pulled up in front of an exquisite apartment house. With its fashionable red brick exterior and a discreet brass nameplate by the front door, it reminded Chelsie of an expensive French restaurant she had once gone to. "The Bradford Arms" simply reeked of wealth, in a quiet, understated way.

"Well, we're there—home sweet home," he announced in an easy voice, a voice that defied the tension that suddenly filled the air between them.

Drew got out of the Mercedes and came around to the door on the passenger's side. He swung it open and peered inside at Chelsie, who was sitting there stiff-backed and stiff-lipped.

"Aren't you coming in?" he asked in a dry tone. Chelsie slowly turned her head and gave him a telling look. "You're safe with me, honey—I promise," Drew said quietly.

Chelsie raised one expressive brow. "I've no doubt of that," she replied, the first reference either of them had made even indirectly to the odd truce they had agreed upon the previous weekend. But that wasn't what was bothering her. She suddenly had the distinct feeling Drew Bradford was far wealthier than she had imagined, and it made her uncomfortable—terribly uncomfortable.

Somewhat less than graciously, Chelsie accepted the hand extended to her and stepped from the car. As they reached the front entrance of the building, a uniformed doorman rushed to greet them.

"Hello, Mr. Bradford," he said familiarly.

"Hello, Austin," Drew returned with a brief smile. He handed over the keys to his Mercedes in a casual ceremony. "Would you please have John park the car and bring up our luggage?"

"Right away, Mr. Bradford," replied the man, with a tip of his hat.

One quick, quiet elevator ride later Chelsie stood on the threshold of Drew's top-floor apartment. Her initial impression was one of elegance and formality. Breathtaking in their authentic eighteenth-century Georgian style, the large off-white, antique-filled rooms were in marked contrast to Drew's cabin in Oneonta. This was a place of family portraits done in oils and crystal chandeliers and elegant "little" dinners. It was as foreign to Chelsie as any foreign country could be. She was definitely out of her element in this high society world, and Drew's apartment only served to emphasize that fact. She wondered which represented the real Drew Bradford—the rustic cabin nestled in the woods or the elegant residence laid out before her.

"Would you like to freshen up and then join me for a glass of wine while we wait for John to bring the luggage?" inquired the man in question.

"Yes, that would be nice," she murmured, wishing nothing more than to be alone for a few minutes. She suddenly felt as though she had agreed to spend the weekend with a stranger.

In the marbled bathroom off the guest room, Chelsie lingered over repairs to her makeup and hair as long as she dared. After giving herself a good talking to, she found her self-confidence, and more important, her sense of humor returning. Just as clothes did not make the man, neither did a few sticks of furniture, she reminded herself.

With her head held a little higher, she went in search of Drew. She found him in the kitchen struggling with a tray of antipasto.

"Here—let me do that," she laughed, taking the platter from his hands. "This looks delicious!" she exclaimed as she examined the contents of the tray. In addition to the traditional anchovies and a variety of olives and meats, there were cold crab and Rock Island shrimp, fresh vegetables and several kinds of sauces for dipping.

Drew stood back and watched as she efficiently

dealt with the plastic wrap that had given him so much
trouble. "I thought we might get hungry before the
party tonight, and dinner seemed out of the question,
considering the time," he remarked. "I arranged for a
local delicatessen to send this over," he added, with a
touch of modesty.

"Why don't you bring the glasses and the wine and
I'll take the tray?" directed Chelsie, as she headed for
a cozy Florida room she had spotted off the formal
living room. She set the tray of antipasto on a
glass-topped table in front of the chintz sofa and took a
seat. "This was very thoughtful, Drew," she murmured, genuinely touched by his concern. Then she
flashed him a bright smile. "Besides—I'm starved!"

"No one can deny you have a healthy appetite,
honey," he drawled, pouring their wine. There was
just the slightest flash of white teeth to give him
away.

Chelsie chose to ignore the innuendo and instead
speared a small piece of crab with a toothpick and
popped it into her mouth. She chewed politely for
some seconds and then took a sip of wine, running her
tongue along her bottom lip in a provocative move
that did not fail to capture her companion's attention.

"It's delicious—you really should try some," she
said in a husky voice, determined to pay him back in
full measure for his pointed reference to her "appetite."

Drew slid an arm along the back of the sofa, his eyes
a flash of lightning against a stormy sky. "I don't know
which tempts me more, sweetheart—you or the antipasto," he murmured, taking a nibble of her ear.

"You'd better have something to eat. It's going to be
a long evening," Chelsie reminded him, offering a

plump ripe olive in her stead. "Now tell me seriously
—just who am I going to meet at this party tonight?"

Entering the party on Drew's arm later that evening,
Chelsie realized how beside the point her question had
been. As a matter of fact, it would have made more
sense to ask who *wasn't* going to be there. For several
hundred people in formal evening dress milled about
the stately home of Richard and Caroline Allen. Thank
God, she had thought to commit to memory the
names of her host and hostess and several key figures
from Bradford Electronics who Drew had informed
her would be in attendance. Otherwise, she was sure
to have remembered none of their names. One good
thing about a gathering this size, speculated Chelsie,
no one would notice if she chose to stir her coffee with
her thumb—if they even served coffee at these upper-
crust affairs.

They had no sooner made their way into the
immense front hall of the Allen home then a beautifully dressed woman of perhaps forty and an equally
impressive man stepped forward to formally greet
them.

"Drew—we're delighted you could come," said the
woman, in a perfectly modulated voice.

"How are you, Caroline? Richard?" Drew responded with a kiss for the woman and a warm handshake
for the man. "I would like you both to meet a special
friend of mine—Dr. Chelsie McBride," he continued,
slipping an arm about Chelsie's waist. "Darling—our
hosts for this evening, Caroline and Richard Allen."

"Dr. McBride—we're so pleased to meet you,"
murmured Caroline Allen, extending a diamond-
encrusted hand in her direction.

"It was kind of you to invite me," Chelsie replied. *Had* the Allens invited her? she wondered. "Please, do call me Chelsie," she added to cover her embarrassment.

"All right, I will, Chelsie," laughed her hostess. "I understand from Drew that you're a college professor. How rare to meet a woman with beauty *and* brains. I hope we have the opportunity to talk more before the evening is over. It's difficult sometimes at a large affair like this."

"I would look forward to it," murmured the younger woman, as she and Drew moved on into the large formal room beyond.

"That wasn't so bad now, was it?" Drew whispered close to her ear.

"Oh, Drew—" Chelsie laughed, her tone only half humorous. "That's like being congratulated after one lap of the Indianapolis 500."

Drew pulled her closer against him. "God, you're shaking like a leaf! There's no reason for you to be nervous, sweetheart. You're the most beautiful woman in the room," he said right out loud, complimenting her as he rarely did when they were alone. "Don't you know that I'm the envy of every man here, Dr. McBride?"

Chelsie felt herself blush beneath his openly sensuous gaze. "I didn't realize you had the gift of the blarney, Drew Bradford. Now behave yourself— someone is headed straight for us!"

Drew looked up and immediately took on a stern, businesslike expression. "Good evening, Walt."

"Hello, Drew. I didn't know if you had made it back to town this weekend or not," the man began, with more than a passing interest in Chelsie. He was obviously waiting for an introduction.

"Darling, this is Walter Fairhurst, president of Bradford Electronics. Walt—Dr. Chelsie McBride."

"*Acting* president of Bradford Electronics," the man quickly corrected Drew. "How do you do, Dr. McBride?"

"Mr. Fairhurst," she replied, with a polite nod.

"Will you be in the office tomorrow, Drew?" Walter Fairhurst reverted to business without further ado. "There are several points concerning that government contract I would like to discuss with you."

"I should be in around ten, Walt. I've arranged for Dr. McBride to tour the facilities. We can talk for a few minutes then."

The other man finally broke down and smiled. "Thanks, Drew. It was a pleasure, doctor. I know my wife will want to meet you. Emily is flitting around here somewhere," he laughed apologetically. Then, his mission accomplished, Walter Fairhurst disappeared into the crowd.

"What an intense little man!" Chelsie blurted out the first thought that came to mind.

"Yes, Walter Fairhurst is one reason I have to make up my mind about Bradford Electronics—and soon," Drew stated, a frown creasing his forehead. "Walt is a good man, but he lacks the initiative it takes to be a top-notch executive. If I decide to get out of the picture permanently, the Board of Directors will be free to offer the position of presidency to any number of up-and-coming young men." Then with a shake of his head, as though he were throwing off an invisible mantle of responsibility, Drew turned to her with a crooked smile. "C'mon honey, let's get a drink. After all, this is supposed to be a party."

Side by side they made their way through the crowd to one of several temporary bars set up in the Allens' home. Chelsie rigidly stuck to ginger ale, feeling a clear head would be required of her if she were to get through this evening with even a modicum of success. For Drew's sake, as well as her own, she intended for it to *be* a success.

She had not told Drew how much she disliked large cocktail parties, but she did, intensely. Anything but an extrovert, she found these affairs a chore under the best of circumstances. She had never been to one yet where the conversation didn't center around "shop" talk. Her personal preference was a small, intimate gathering of friends, where people could really talk to each other.

And wasn't that the purpose of this weekend? For her and Drew to get to know each other better? She failed to see how that could be accomplished in a crowd of several hundred people.

Then Chelsie's attention was once more required as a group of people seemed to form around herself and Drew. She tried to catch as many first names as she could, quickly recognizing that last names were beyond her. There was that rather nice redhead and her husband. And then some terribly chic blonde who had clung to Drew as if she couldn't stand on her own two feet without his support. Chelsie smiled and made inane conversation, not one word of which she could recall later. Then an apparent break came and she decided that a visit to the powder room was in order. Her head was starting to ache already.

With the directions given to her by Drew, Chelsie

was able to successfully locate the powder room on the first try. She did give her appearance a once-over, but her real reason for slipping away from the crowd was to have a few minutes of peace and quiet in which to recoup her forces. Recognizing the origin of the tension headache coming on, she downed several of the aspirin she carried in her evening bag. Then, with no further excuses to delay her, she made her way back to the party.

When she walked back into the Allens' living room it was only to discover that Drew Bradford was nowhere in sight. Fighting down a feeling of momentary panic, Chelsie ordered another ginger ale to give her hands something to hold on to. Well—she was not about to wander from room to room in search of the blasted man. She had her pride, too. After all, she was a grown woman, not some lost sheep without a shepherd.

Settling on the edge of one particularly talkative group, Chelsie tried to look like she somehow belonged in this glittering display of designer-name gowns and formal black tuxedos.

"You're with Andrew, aren't you, my dear?" said a matronly woman, who seemed more friendly than the others. "I'm Helen Whitman, a friend of Charlotte's— Drew's mother," she explained, seeing the puzzlement on the girl's face.

"How do you do, Mrs. Whitman. I'm Chelsie McBride," she spoke up, grateful for the woman's interest.

"What a pretty little thing you are, Miss McBride. Are you a model or something?"

"No, I'm not a model," Chelsie answered hesitantly.

"What a pity," sighed the older woman, for what reason Chelsie could not imagine. "What do you do, then?" Helen Whitman asked rather pointedly.

"I'm a college professor. I teach medieval literature, primarily Chaucer," Chelsie supplied, probably a little too eagerly, but here was the first person to show any real interest in her all evening.

"Chaucer—"

And just by the way the woman repeated the word, Chelsie knew Helen Whitman had no idea who Geoffrey Chaucer was. "I teach English literature, Mrs. Whitman," she clarified, with a small sigh.

"How nice! Such a good occupation for a woman, don't you think, Miss McBride?"

"Yes, I do," Chelsie replied, ready to settle down to a banal exchange on the merits of being a teacher.

Chelsie managed to steer her away from that topic of conversation, only to find herself being regaled for the next half hour with stories of Helen Whitman's grandchildren, ages four and five. When the first opportune moment presented itself, the younger woman politely excused herself.

But her freedom was short-lived, as a brittle, high-pitched female voice caught Chelsie's attention.

"Well . . . well . . . if it isn't the little schoolteacher!" The same champagne-blonde who had draped herself all over Drew earlier now stood planted directly in Chelsie's path.

The woman had obviously had too much to drink. Chelsie knew from experience that it was better to avoid a confrontation under those circumstances.

"Hello, Miss Wells." She tried to smile, glad at least to have remembered the woman's name, but couldn't quite manage it in the end. She nonchalantly tried instead to make her way past the woman.

"Are you a *real* doctor?" The woman demanded in a belligerent voice.

"I'm not a medical doctor, if that's what you mean. I do have a Ph.d.," Chelsie replied conversationally.

The blonde's laugh was an insult in itself. "How novel of Drew to pick a woman with brains instead of beauty for a change."

"Apparently so," said Chelsie, giving tit for tat. She knew people were beginning to stare at them, but she was not about to let Monica Wells make mincemeat out of her.

The other woman's dark eyes were full of malice. "What do you do to keep Drew interested, Dr. McBride? Read to him in bed?"

Chelsie had an odd and rather unpleasant feeling in her stomach. She had never had to deal with a jealous drunk before. Perhaps honesty was still the best policy even in a case like this.

"I can only assume your tasteless remark is due to the fact you have had too much to drink, Miss Wells," she said, her voice displaying controlled calmness.

"Are you trying to make me look like a fool?" Monica Wells demanded in a slurred tone, obviously voicing the words with difficulty.

Chelsie told herself to stay calm. There was no point in surrendering to fear, and no point in retreat, she decided, taking the offensive.

"I don't have to *try* to make you look like a fool, Miss Wells. You're doing that quite well without any help from me."

"Ah, knock it off, Monica!" A bored male voice came from the sidelines.

The man's words seemed to act like a trigger release. With her mouth twisted most unattractively and with fists clenched, the woman renewed her attack.

"How long do you think you can hold on to a man like Drew with all that intellectual nonsense? That's not what a man wants from a woman," sneered the blonde. "Did Drew tell you about me, doctor?"

There was no dignity in a situation like this, but Chelsie was determined to retain what little she could. She could feel everyone's eyes on her, waiting for her to retaliate in kind.

"Before tonight I had never heard your name, Miss Wells. Apparently, Drew didn't feel it was worth mentioning," she said in a soft, but firm voice.

The other woman's face became suffused with color. "Why you little . . . who do you think you are?"

"Dr. McBride is an honored guest in my home," came the clear, bell-like voice of Caroline Allen. Their hostess stepped forward to stand beside Chelsie, her eyes never leaving the astonished face of Monica Wells for a moment. "You seem a little under the weather, Monica. I'll have someone drive you home." With a regal nod of her head, Caroline Allen dismissed the woman. Then she turned to Chelsie with a smile of encouragement, slipping a supportive arm through the younger woman's. "Come along with me, Chelsie. So many people have been asking to meet you, including the senator." Guiding her gracefully through the crowd, Caroline smiled as brightly as if nothing unpleasant had occurred. "That's the girl!" she whispered to Chelsie. "Keep that chin up until I get us out of here."

"Oh, Caroline—I'm so sorry about what happened," Chelsie murmured fervently.

"I should be the one apologizing to you, my dear. To think that one of my guests should actually be abused in my home." The woman shook her head, looking distraught. "You can believe Monica Wells won't be welcome here in the future. She's gone too far this time."

"I don't think she meant it, Caroline. She had obviously had too much to drink."

"You are far too generous with her, Chelsie. This isn't the first time I've witnessed one of Monica's little scenes. She is *persona non grata* as of tonight. Let's slip in here, shall we?" Caroline Allen indicated a quiet, empty study off the hallway. "What we need is a good strong drink—for medicinal purposes, of course." She handed Chelsie just that and took one for herself before she settled on the sofa beside her guest.

"I feel guilty," said Chelsie, taking a sip of her drink. "You shouldn't be sitting here consoling me, Caroline. You have a whole houseful of guests to see to out there."

"They can see to themselves for a few minutes," the woman said, apparently unconcerned. "We deserve a break—both of us."

"Well, thank you for coming to my rescue. You handled the situation beautifully."

"Thank you." Caroline acknowledged the compliment by touching her glass to Chelsie's in a toast. "To us—may we always overcome." Then the two smiled at each other conspiratorially. "Other than that run-in with Monica Wells, are you enjoying yourself?" inquired the older woman.

"I have enjoyed meeting you and your husband," Chelsie responded with care, not wishing to actually lie.

"I see—I wonder why Drew chose to bring you here for the first time tonight. We don't always entertain in these numbers, you know," Caroline said thoughtfully.

"Perhaps he wanted to see how I handled myself in a crowd," Chelsie suggested.

"Well, you've handled yourself beautifully and I intend to tell him so myself. Do you think you're ready to face that crowd again?"

"I think so," Chelsie replied with more bravado than she actually felt.

"I knew you were a woman of spirit the minute I met you, Dr. Chelsie McBride," Caroline said, as they left the study. "I wonder if Drew realizes he has finally met his match."

Chelsie would have loved to ask her hostess to explain that last comment, but they were back in the midst of the party by then and the very man they had been discussing was coming toward them.

"Caroline—Chelsie." Drew said their names in greeting. "What in the dickens have you two been up to?"

"We just sneaked away for a quiet drink," Caroline explained without explaining. "Chelsie has been enchanting my guests one and all, I might add. If you bring her to Albany very often, she's going to be in great demand, Drew." Chelsie nearly choked on that one. "Now I've promised the senator that he will be the next person to meet Dr. McBride. So, come along, my dear Chelsie," Caroline said breezily, as only she could. "You can tag along, too, if you wish, Drew."

Somehow Andrew Bradford wasn't as pleased by all of this as either woman had thought he would be. In fact, he appeared almost displeased. But neither Caroline nor Chelsie relented. To their way of thinking, it was the least he deserved for leaving Chelsie on her own for the greater part of the evening.

"I'm sorry I was gone for so long, honey," Drew whispered to the woman at his side as they both followed Caroline Allen across the room.

"Were you gone a long time?" Chelsie said, with all the innocence she could muster.

"You know damned well I've practically ignored you all evening," growled the man, indicting himself in the process.

"You said it, Drew—not me," Chelsie replied bitterly, no longer able to hide her feelings from him. "You're guilty as charged on that count and a great deal more!"

Then Caroline Allen was introducing the senator from New York and Andrew Bradford unhappily remained in the dark as to what else he might be guilty of.

7

~oooooooooo~

She was dreaming. It was a wild, wonderful dream from which she hoped never to awaken. For Drew was holding her in his embrace as though he would never let her go, kissing her with unbridled passion, caressing her with hands that seemed to know every secret her body possessed. It was a dream born of passion. And from the depths of her soul she responded with all the love and desire she had for this man, her body arching into his, seeking the satisfaction only he could offer.

It was there in her dreams that she first discovered she loved Drew—loved him as a woman hopes to love a man once in her lifetime. Chelsie cried out his name. She did not want to wake up. She wanted to be left alone to go on dreaming forever. But something or someone kept insisting that she open her eyes.

She struggled out of sleep only to find she was

indeed being kissed quite thoroughly by Drew Bradford as he bent over her bed. This was certainly better than her usual alarm clock, she thought, as he dropped another kiss on her mouth.

"Good morning, sleepyhead," he murmured, making a production of sitting down on the edge of the mattress. "I brought you a cup of coffee." Drew tacked that on as an afterthought, as if he had forgotten the coffee himself in the aftermath of their passion.

"Hm—thank you," Chelsie yawned in a sleep-rusty voice, stretching her arms high above her head as she sat up. Little did she realize that her action pulled the silky nightgown taut across her breasts, outlining their tempting form in erotic detail. It was an unconscious act of seduction, if she had but known.

"I *was* going to offer you a cup of coffee," the man breathed in a husky tone, "but you've given me a far better idea. . . ."

Then he kissed her again—deeply, passionately, and Chelsie found the reality of his kiss far more devastating to her senses than a dream could ever be. This time when Drew pulled away she saw the carefully masked desire in his eyes and knew that he wanted her here and now. The knowledge sent a strange thrill coursing through her.

She inhaled a slow, trembling breath. "What about my coffee?"

A look of faint amusement crossed his face. "I'll reheat it for you later," he said in a low voice, his gaze dropping to the rapid rise and fall of her breasts.

As if he were held by some mysterious spell, Drew slowly reached out to trace the rounded swell of one breast. He drew a line back and forth with his finger, watching with fascination as a small peak formed beneath her gown.

Chelsie considered voicing a word or two in protest, but his touch felt so good she seemed to forget every rational thought she had ever had. Instead, she found herself holding her breath as he continued his sensuous caresses. Chelsie could deny her feelings no longer. She let out a low, animallike moan and reached for him.

He came to her then eagerly, knowing that she wanted him. His mouth found hers in a searing kiss that swept away the last vestiges of sleep as nothing else could. His tongue opened her lips, already warm and willing, and he plunged into her without thought of the inevitable chain of events he was setting in motion.

Chelsie wrapped her arms about his waist, wishing that his robe would somehow miraculously disappear. She wanted to touch him, to give fully to him the same pleasure he so generously gave to her, to feel his flesh beneath her fingertips.

Suddenly she knew that nothing else mattered—not last night, not Monica Wells, not even the strained abstinence of the past two weeks—nothing mattered but this wonderful thing that was happening between the two of them. All else was but a shadowy dream beside the intense pleasure of this moment.

Then Drew was pulling away from her, and in her disappointment at the loss of his warmth, she cried out his name once more.

"Drew—" Chelsie heard the plea in her own voice.

"I know, honey—but dammit, I need you," he swore, seeming to misinterpret her plea. "To hell with nobility!" he muttered, untying the bathrobe and letting it slip to the floor. He pulled back the covers and eased himself down onto the bed beside her, gently taking her into his arms.

This was as Chelsie had dreamed. The feel of the hard male body next to hers, clearly outlined against her own silk-clad form, was heavenly. If only Drew loved her . . . if only it could be this way every morning for the rest of her life. . . .

Thus began the most erotic search she had experienced in her twenty-eight years. Drew used the silky nightgown as a sensuous tool, tracing every curve and valley of her body through its flimsy covering, setting her ablaze until she nearly pleaded with him to take her.

But her need remained unvoiced as she took action of her own. Chelsie responded with her hands, making little forays down his body as she rediscovered the small hollow beneath his ribs, the firm, muscular thigh, the sprinkling of dark hair down the front of his torso. Drew reacted as she had known—had hoped—that he would, with the fierce evidence of his desire rising up to meet her eager touch. She caressed him with all the love and tenderness in her heart, learning the ways to give him pleasure as she went.

Drew responded in kind until Chelsie felt as though she were all feeling. His mouth was warm and sweet in its demands, demands she rushed to meet, satisfying her own needs at the same time. She felt him slip the straps of her nightgown from her shoulders, and then the two pink breasts were laid bare for his gaze and his exploration.

Drew bent over her, finding the tip of one ripe nipple with his teeth. He tugged gently again and again, torturing her with an exquisite pain born of pleasure. Then the next thing Chelsie knew Drew had rolled beneath her and she was being lifted above him. He held her there, her breasts within easy reach of his tongue and lips and teeth. He seemed intent on devouring all of her with his mouth as he tasted the sensuous delights her body offered.

His strong hands spanned her waist, caressed the curve of her thigh, the hollow in the small of her back, until she was molten lava in the heat of their passion. Then she was once more stretched out beneath him, in anticipation of their mutual need to find in each other the best part of themselves.

"Drew, I love you," Chelsie whispered as his mouth was crushed to hers.

"Oh, babe—I want you, too," he said in a muffled groan, as he cleared a pathway between her legs with his own. "I need you now," he breathed against the softness of her breast.

For one stunned instant, Chelsie could not find her breath as Drew drove home the proof of that need. Then her own desire to give and receive overpowered every other sensation and she eagerly joined him in the quest for their mutual fulfillment. It was a fulfillment sought and found as never before there in each other's arms. In the aftermath of their passionate lovemaking, she curled up contentedly beside him and drifted into a dreamless sleep.

Drew was the first to rouse in answer to the persistent buzzing of a doorbell somewhere in the distance. Chelsie rolled over on her stomach and watched through half-open lids as he swung his legs over the edge of the bed and sat up.

"Damn! What time is it?" he muttered, flinging himself off the bed. In one fluid movement, he swept the bathrobe off the floor and was out the door of her bedroom.

Voices drifted back to Chelsie from the front hallway as Drew spoke briefly to another man. She was sitting up with the sheet tucked around her when he returned only minutes later. He stood at the foot of the bed and looked down at her, his attitude clearly one of impatience.

"C'mon, honey—we have to get a move on it. That was my driver informing me my car is waiting. We're supposed to be at Bradford Electronics in a half hour. Can you be ready in fifteen minutes?"

"Ready—no," she laughed dryly, "but I can be dressed in fifteen minutes."

The moment Drew closed the bedroom door behind him, Chelsie scurried off the bed and began to dress as if the devil himself were on her heels.

"I hope I have all my clothes on," she muttered to Drew as they walked through the front doors of the impressive office building in downtown Albany.

"You look beautiful with or without your clothes on," Drew murmured in her ear as he guided her into the elevator. Then a mask seemed to fall into place on his handsome features as Chelsie once more witnessed the transformation from private man to public executive. "You will be meeting my administrative assistant, Maggie Reardon, this morning. She's agreed to take you on a tour of the facilities while I meet with Walt Fairhurst." He spoke the words in a clipped tone, as if he were reading from a schedule.

Chelsie caught the tip of her tongue between her teeth and permitted herself a small sigh. "Couldn't I just wait for you in an office somewhere until your meeting is over?" She paused and added wistfully, "I'd much rather *you* took me on the tour of your company."

Drew contemplated her without any change in expression. "I wish I could, but I don't know how long my meeting with Fairhurst will last. There's no sense in your waiting around for an hour or two. Besides, Maggie Reardon knows as much about Bradford Electronics as I do. You'll be in good hands."

"I'm sure I will," she muttered, letting her arms fall in a classic gesture of defeat. The point was that she wanted to be in *his* hands, not some assistant's she had never met before. But the look on Drew's impassive face told her that any objections she might make would be futile. They were in his world now and apparently here he was indeed boss.

The elevator quietly came to a stop at the tenth and top floor of the Bradford Building. Chelsie knew that these were the executive office suites—Drew had informed her of that much. The receptionist behind the front desk respectfully said, "Good morning, Mr. Bradford," as they walked past her to his office. There, boldly lettered on the door, was the name Andrew Bradford.

Drew opened the outer door and stepped back to let Chelsie enter first. It was indeed an impressive room with its paneled walls, thick carpeting, and expensive furniture. It took Chelsie a moment to realize that this wasn't Drew's office at all, but his secretary's.

"Good morning, Ruth," he said in brisk greeting.

"Good morning, Andrew," returned the efficient-looking, middle-aged woman, as she rose to her feet.

Chelsie halfway expected the woman to salute, but, of course, she did no such thing.

"Chelsie, I would like you to meet my secretary, Mrs. Ruth Halliday. Ruth, this is Dr. Chelsie McBride. Dr. McBride is here to tour Bradford Electronics." Without further explanation, he got down to business. "I have a meeting with Walt in five minutes. Will you pull those government contracts he wants to go over? Then call Maggie and tell her to meet Dr. McBride in this office in five minutes."

"There are a number of telephone messages on your desk, Andrew. I've noted the ones I think you should try to return even though it is Saturday," Ruth Halliday stated judiciously.

"I'll see how many I can get to," Drew replied, without making any promises. He stepped into the next room, motioning Chelsie to follow.

If she had thought his secretary's office was impressive, it definitely paled in comparison to the one she now stood in. Here then was the setting of Andrew Bradford, the successful executive. With its oversized hand-carved desk, original oil paintings hanging on the walls, and even a wood-burning fireplace in one corner, the office was unlike anything Chelsie had seen before. She was still trying to take in the opulence of her surroundings when Drew walked over to her and dropped a light kiss on her mouth.

"Enjoy your tour with Maggie, honey. I'll meet you back here for lunch in about two hours. Make yourself at home," he called over one shoulder. Then Drew was gone before Chelsie could say a word.

Chelsie felt a little like a bride left waiting at the altar. As she stood there alone in Drew Bradford's office, she had good reason to ask herself what on God's earth she was doing there. This world of opulence and power and money wasn't her world and never could be. But she was beginning to see that it was Drew's, and would indeed continue to be Drew's, if in the end he chose to remain at Bradford Electronics.

It was then that she realized that she might well be in love with a man she could never really have—not that he had asked her to have him. In fact, Drew had not said "love" that morning in response to her own declaration, but "want." And there was a world of difference between the two.

She felt a sharp pain between her ribs like a knife being twisted and turned in her flesh. She had been a fool to think that all that mattered was the two of them and the passion they shared. It wasn't enough. Sometimes in the end even love was not enough.

Chelsie was standing by the window looking out at a tenth-floor view of Albany, lost in her own thoughts unwillingly and unhappily, when the low, cultured accents of a woman's voice reached her ears.

"Dr. McBride?"

She slowly turned around and saw a sophisticated and very feminine woman posed in the doorway of Drew's office.

"Yes—" Chelsie acknowledged quietly.

"I am Margo Reardon, Dr. McBride—Drew's administrative assistant." The tall, dark-haired woman came forward to shake her hand in a distinctly businesslike manner.

"I'm pleased to meet you, Miss Reardon," Chelsie replied, setting her mouth into some semblance of a smile.

Close up, Chelsie was surprised to discover that this woman could not be her senior by more than a year or two. It was the sophisticated, swept-back hair style, she determined, that had initially misled her. With her dark hair and equally dark eyes set against a porcelain complexion, Margo Reardon was without a doubt one of the loveliest women she had ever seen. Dressed in an expensive ultrasuede suit in a shade of deep blue, Drew's assistant was the epitome of the well-heeled woman executive.

"I have been informed that you would like to tour our facilities here," the woman continued politely. "Since Drew is busy elsewhere, I will be happy to show you around and explain whatever I can."

Chelsie permitted herself a small sigh. "That's very kind of you, Miss Reardon. I'm sure you're a busy woman."

"I'm only too pleased to do Drew a special favor when he requests it," Margo replied with her first smile—a smile no doubt brought on by the mere mention of the man's name. "Shall we get started, Dr. McBride? We have a great deal to see if I am to have you back here in two hours." She motioned to Chelsie that she should precede her out the door.

"Thank you," Chelsie said, with a slight inclination of her head, going on ahead of the woman.

"I think we'll go down to the first floor and work our way back up," Margo proposed, as she rang for the elevator. "We have a number of departments housed in the Bradford Building—sales, marketing, industrial relations, finance, legal, and research and development, plus two floors of offices and the dining room. Research and development has just about outgrown its facilities here. That's Drew's personal baby, and he'll have to decide soon where he's going to move it."

"Is that his decision alone?" Chelsie heard herself ask. "I understood that kind of decision was handled by a company's board of directors."

"Bradford Electonics is a private corporation, Dr. McBride, not a public one. As such, its stock is held by a relatively small number of shareholders. It is a well-known fact that Drew retains control of fifty-one percent himself, while Charlotte Bradford has control of another sizable portion. Yes, we have a board of directors, but on paper and in spirit Drew Bradford *is* this company." Margo Reardon's voice rang with conviction. She was obviously proud of the company and the man.

"I see. . . ." Chelsie murmured, drawing her delicate brows together. She wasn't at all sure that she liked what she was hearing from this woman. She saw no place in this scheme of things for *Professor* Andrew Bradford. "And what of Drew's desire to teach?" she felt compelled to ask.

Margo Reardon deliberated for several minutes before she answered. "Naturally, we all understand that Drew is torn right now between his responsibility to the company and his personal desire to teach. But I have every confidence he will make the right decision in the end." The woman apparently thought she knew what that decision would be. "Now—let's start here in the sales department. Of course, there will be some things I can't explain in detail, and with this being a Saturday, there will be only a few people in the building. I'm sure Drew can fill you in later if you have questions I can't answer."

Chelsie was quite sure she would have questions for Drew but not of a technical nature. She gave Margo a nod to go ahead, and off they went on their tour of Bradford Electronics.

About an hour and three-quarters later, her head already swimming with facts and figures, Chelsie was trying to absorb Margo Reardon's lecture on the current projects of the research and development department.

"Yes—Drew has us rather heavily into microchips and fiber optics at the moment," she was saying, as if Chelsie would naturally know what microchips and fiber optics were. "In Drew's opinion, microchips are going to be the real wave of the future. After all, doctor, just think of all the technology that uses microchips to store information—computers, word processors, and the rapidly growing market of home computers."

"And fiber optics?" Chelsie said after a companionable silence, trying to appear intelligent.

"We're working on that in conjunction with the telephone companies, of course. I'm sure you know that it's an underground fiber or cable that uses a beam of light to transmit, rather than the current wire," Margo explained in her brisk, businesslike way.

"Yes, I see," murmured Chelsie. She didn't see, of course, but she was not about to admit that to Margo Reardon. The woman might actually try to explain, and any explanation—no matter how elementary—would be of no earthly use to Chelsie. She had never been mechanically inclined. If one wanted to discuss the French influences in Chaucer's work or the medieval idea of courtly love, then she was on solid ground.

But all this technical talk was strictly mumbo jumbo to her.

"Well, I see our time is nearly up," stated Margo, with a quick glance at her watch. "Why don't we check in with Ruth and find out if Drew has concluded his meeting? I'd be very surprised if he has." A knowing smile appeared on the woman's lovely face. "The cafeteria is closed on Saturdays, but I can offer you a cup of coffee in my office."

"I would love a cup of coffee," Chelsie said, with the first real enthusiasm she had felt all morning. "We got up too late to have any coffee this morning." She immediately bit her lip and looked away for a moment, fervently hoping that Margo Reardon had missed her reference to "we." Apparently she had, for Chelsie noticed no sign of awareness in the other woman's expression when she once more faced her.

As his assistant had suspected, Drew was still tied up with Walter Fairhurst, and so the two women proceeded to Margo's office for coffee. They settled themselves in a comfortable arrangement of chairs with their coffee before the conversation was picked up again.

"Tell me, Dr. McBride—" the woman hesitated, appearing unsure of herself for the first time. "Would it be impertinent of me to call you Chelsie?"

"Good heavens, no!" her companion laughed lightly. "I've been trying to think of a way all morning to get past Dr. McBride and Miss Reardon."

"You met Drew at the college in Oneonta, didn't you, Chelsie?" Margo asked uneasily.

"Yes, I did," Chelsie answered, waiting to see just what direction Drew's assistant was headed with her questioning.

Margo Reardon started to say something, then changed her mind. "I've worked for Bradford Electronics in one capacity or another for eight years, Chelsie. For the past four I've been in the enviable position of being Drew's administrative assistant. I've watched and worked alongside him as he built this company into what it is today—a leader in the electronics field."

Margo paused for a moment, as if to gather her thoughts. Impatient as she was for the woman to get to the point, Chelsie was careful not to interrupt those thoughts.

When she was ready, Margo went on—but her voice had softened. She seemed less remote somehow, more human, more a woman. "I've seen Drew Bradford struggle with numerous problems in those years, but none has compared to the struggle he is going through now. I suppose what I'm trying to ask you is whether he seems happy teaching at the state university."

Margo surprised her. Wherever Chelsie had thought this was all leading, she hadn't expected that. Happy —what a strange choice of words for a business colleague to use. Then she looked at the lovely, sophisticated woman beside her and knew that the interest was more than professional.

"I'm not sure I can answer that question," Chelsie began, struggling to express herself. "Drew is a different man here than he is in Oneonta. There he's more relaxed, he laughs more—he even seems younger, somehow. I think Drew genuinely likes to teach, but if you're asking me if I think he can give up all of this—" She gestured broadly with her hands as if to encompass the whole of Bradford Electronics. "I don't know.

I don't think Drew knows." She took a deep breath and finished almost sadly. "He told me once he didn't know if he could just walk away from it."

"Drew may think that he can and he might even try it for a while—but if he does, he'll regret that decision in the end," Margo staunchly declared, then came straight to the point. "And he will resent anyone who forced him to make the wrong choice."

"I can't imagine Drew allowing himself to be *forced* to do anything, can you?" Chelsie said, equally blunt.

The woman beside her leaned forward suddenly and looked Chelsie straight in the eyes. "We both know force can take many forms, Dr. McBride, some more subtle than others. I want what is best for both Drew and Bradford Electronics."

Chelsie's eyes did not falter. "And are you so sure that you know what is best?" she asked in a gentle tone. "In the end, it won't matter what either one of us thinks, you know. The decision will be Drew's and Drew's alone."

"I don't think you actually believe that any more than I do," Margo said, not unkindly. She was clearly resolute in her determination to convince the other woman that as Drew's assistant she did know best.

"Drew and I are friends." There was the slightest hesitation in Chelsie's voice as she said that last word. "I think you are overestimating the influence I have over him."

"I don't think I am," Margo said, seeming to choose her words with care. "Do you know you are the only woman 'friend' Drew Bradford has ever actually invited to these offices? I thought not," she murmured, interpreting the surprised look on Chelsie's face. "Oh, there were several women, like Monica Wells, who took it upon themselves to drop in. They didn't last long with Drew after that. The minute he mentioned that he was bringing you here, I knew what it meant," she said in a low, earnest voice. "You have a great deal of influence with Drew whether you know it or not, Dr. McBride."

"And you're afraid—" Chelsie groped for the right word, "you're concerned—that I will use that influence to persuade him to leave Bradford Electronics?"

Margo Reardon studied her intently for a moment. "Wouldn't you? Can you honestly say you would be happy in Drew's world if that world were Bradford Electronics?"

"No—I can't say that," Chelsie replied in a flat voice.

"Then do you really think Drew would be happy for long in your world?" Margo asked, following up her advantage.

Chelsie listened to her as if she resented every word the woman spoke. She closed her eyes and tried to think. "I don't know," she finally conceded, more confused than angry. "I just don't know."

"You're a beautiful and intelligent woman, Chelsie McBride, and I wish Drew had never met you. You're going to hurt him badly no matter what you decide."

Stunned by Margo's indictment and half afraid that it was true, Chelsie sat there at a loss for words. After all, what could she say to this woman—that she was sorry Margo felt that way about her?

The unnatural silence between the two women stretched into a minute and then two until it was finally shattered by the harsh ring of the telephone on Margo Reardon's desk. She set her coffee cup down and quickly rose to answer the call. Just by the tone of her voice, Chelsie knew it was Drew on the other end.

"Yes—all right, Drew, I'll give her the message," Margo agreed, as she put the receiver down after some minutes. "That was Drew—he won't be able to meet you for lunch. He suggested the two of us go out to eat. Then I could drop you off at his apartment. Apparently, there's a party tonight the two of you will be attending. He said he'd be home in time to change for it." The message was concluded in the same monotone with which it had been delivered.

Chelsie felt the heat rise to her face with each word. Damn the man! Why hadn't he asked to speak to her personally rather than relay his apologies through Margo? While she did not wish to be rude, she had quite frankly had enough of Drew's assistant for one day. The last thing she needed right now was to spend another hour in the woman's company over lunch!

"If you don't mind, I think I'll pass on lunch, Margo," she said, getting to her feet. "I've taken up enough of your time already." Chelsie held out her hand in a gesture of good will. "Thank you for the coffee and for the tour."

"It was my pleasure, Dr. McBride," Margo responded, reverting to her usual polite manner. "I would still be glad to drive you to Drew's," she added.

"Thanks—but I'll grab a cab." Chelsie smiled mechanically.

There was an awkward moment as the two women faced each other in the doorway of Margo Reardon's office—faced each other not as enemies, but as rivals of a far subtler nature.

"Under other circumstances, we might have been

friends, Chelsie," Margo murmured, her eyes dark with regret.

"Yes—we might have," sighed Chelsie. "Goodbye, Margo." Then she turned and walked out of the office, out of the Bradford Building, without once looking back.

All the while she rode in the taxi cab, the driver cheerfully keeping up a nonstop line of chatter—all the while the manager of the Bradford Arms politely arranged to unlock Drew's apartment door for her—Chelsie's one thought was that she wanted to be alone.

And then the moment came at last when she stood by herself in the entranceway of Drew Bradford's apartment. With an irreverence that befitted her mood, she tossed her handbag onto an original eighteenth-century Chippendale chair, kicked off her shoes, and plopped herself down on one of the three sofas in the living room.

Plumping several fat pillows behind her head, Chelsie swung her legs over the end of the sofa and dangled them like a kid. She brooded for a moment, whistling between her teeth. Not ready to face the real problem that confronted her, she set her mind to figuring out why this room bothered her. The furniture was all lovely antiques, no reproductions; the paintings were originals; the decor was obviously done by a professional—in fact, everything about it was perfect. That was the problem—it was too perfect.

Everything had its place and everything was in that place. It was neat and orderly and perfect—and it looked like a room out of *House Beautiful*. Chelsie realized it didn't even appear as if anyone lived here—and perhaps no one did. It was becoming abundantly clear to her that Drew's life style included very little time at home. It seemed to be an endless round of business meetings and parties and more business meetings.

"What kind of life is that?" she heard herself ask aloud.

It wasn't the kind of life she wanted to lead. It wasn't her life now and it never could be. She was a woman of simple pleasures—music, reading, bicycling, and teaching. She had always thought that if she did find the right man to love, he would share those same pleasures. Well—she was in love, but with the wrong man!

Then Chelsie suddenly realized anew that there were times when love was not enough. She loved Drew Bradford, but she could not change who she was, what she was, simply to suit his life style—no more than Drew could change himself to suit hers.

Oh—they could try. She might be able to convince Drew that he could be content in her world, teaching in a college somewhere—anywhere. But Margo Reardon was right, much as she hated to admit it. The day would come when Drew would resent her, perhaps even hate her, for persuading him to try to be something he wasn't.

No human being had the right to expect that of another. To love someone was to accept him as he was, not to try to change him. Chelsie knew then that she would rather leave loving Drew than stay knowing that some day, one day, he might grow to hate her.

And leave she must, she concluded, while she still had the strength to do so. She couldn't wait until Drew got home that evening—for he would only find a way around her protests, as he always did. She must go now before he returned.

Armed with the strength of her convictions, Chelsie McBride forced herself to do just that. She quickly and efficiently packed her bags and even thought to call the bus depot for a schedule of buses running that afternoon to Oneonta. Then came the most difficult part of all. She couldn't just walk out that door without leaving behind some note of explanation for Drew. She wasn't that much of a coward.

There followed the most painful fifteen minutes of Chelsie's life. How did she tell the man that she loved him, but that it would never work out between them? How did she learn to let go of what she had never really had in the first place? In the end, she hastily scribbled a few words on a piece of note paper and left it propped against the mirror in the front hall.

As she walked out of his apartment for the last time, Chelsie McBride knew she was not only turning her back on Drew Bradford, but on part of herself, as well.

8

~oooooooooo~

The bus ride back to Oneonta that afternoon was the longest journey of Chelsie's twenty-eight years. Still, she knew she had made the only decision she could make—for her own sake as well as Drew's. Sometimes it was better to let love go than to stay until it was no longer love.

It didn't take a corporate lawyer to figure out that she and Drew Bradford were the original odd couple. Their worlds were separated by far more than money, Chelsie could see that now. For a brief span of time she had allowed herself to believe that the differences did not matter, but they did. The time to stop kidding herself had come. Perhaps Drew felt the same way and had simply not found the courage to tell her.

Surely he had seen that she didn't belong in his world of Mercedes-Benzes and Gainsboroughs any more than he belonged in her world of homemade clothes and compact cars bought on time. But it was more than material possessions that separated the two of them. It was the intangibles of life, too.

Chelsie knew she was essentially and hopelessly middle class. The life style in which she had been raised, the kind of home her parents had created for their four children, was one in which learning was respected above all else. Success was not measured in material possessions, but in accomplishments. *Doing* was more important than *having*.

Chelsie didn't think about it very often, it seemed such a natural part of her, but if she did marry one day and have children, she would want a husband—and a father for those children—who could give of himself, whose time and energies, as well as his love, would be for his family. Love alone was not enough. She could never be happy with a man whose life was wrapped up in his career to the exclusion of all else.

Marriage was a lifelong commitment to Chelsie. She had seen it work for her parents, but for so many others it had not. And she was too level-headed to be unrealistic about it at her age. Even if Drew had been interested in marrying her—and the subject never had come up between them—she would have had to think long and hard. She wasn't at all sure they were suited for anything beyond a wild and brief affair. The trouble was, she had never thought of herself as the wild-and-brief-affair type.

In her heart, if she would but admit it, Chelsie knew that if she could by some miracle snap her fingers and make Drew into the kind of man who would be content as a college professor—she would do it! She loved him. She wanted a chance at the kind of happiness she could find with him. But the Andrew

Bradford of Bradford Electronics was a different matter altogether. He was a man who enjoyed power. It was his driving ambition that had made his company what it was today—a leader in its field, as Margo Reardon had not hesitated to tell her.

Chelsie wasn't sure she could ever understand what drove a man or woman to seek that kind of success and power. She wanted to be the best teacher she was capable of being—that seemed a worthy goal to her—but to seek power, to desire control over others, to amass great sums of money—she failed to understand those pursuits. It wasn't that she was naive; far from it. She just felt there had to be more to life than that.

But what was life without love? The thought crawled through her brain. And what was her life going to be now that she loved a man she could never be with? She was a fool! She might be able to run away from Drew Bradford, but she couldn't run away from herself. In just a few short weeks, he had managed to become the reason for her existence. It didn't make sense. Sense? Since when had common sense entered into the picture? If she'd had any common sense, she wouldn't have gotten involved with the man in the first place.

These thoughts and more churned round and round in her head on the bus trip back to Oneonta. And as she stood in the living room of her own apartment, home at last, they continued to plague her. She wearily dragged her suitcase into the bedroom and began to unpack. When the last article of clothing had been put away, she finally gave in to the despair that held her in its grip. First one tear fell and then another until they came too fast and too numerous to count. She threw herself down on the bed then and wept long and bitterly, as if her heart were breaking. And indeed it was.

It was late when Chelsie awoke. She sensed it first, then confirmed it with a glance at the clock on the bedside table. She was momentarily disoriented, her head thick and fuzzy. Then it all came rushing back to her—it was Saturday night, and instead of going to the party with Drew she had run away.

She felt awful and knew she must look even worse. Her eyes were sore and puffy, her throat scratchy, her head felt like she had a hangover, and she was hungry.

"God!" groaned Chelsie. How could she feel so miserable and still be hungry? Because she hadn't eaten a thing all day, she reminded herself. It was little wonder she was famished.

She forced herself to sit up, then to stand, and finally to put one foot in front of the other and walk to the kitchen. With automatic movements, she put the tea kettle on and prepared a mug of instant soup. She carried it into the living room and curled up in the big armchair, tucking her feet beneath her. The once smart wool suit she had been so proud of scarcely mattered now. It was already a mass of wrinkles.

At the moment, Chelsie felt like a puppet without any strings, an empty shell. She was numb from head to toe. Her mind was a blank. And there was quiet all around her. She was alone, just as she had wished to be—very alone.

She had no idea how long she sat there. She suddenly realized her soup was gone, but she couldn't remember drinking it. She slowly got to her feet and retraced her steps to the bedroom. She undressed in the dark and slipped into a nightgown. Without putting the light on in the bathroom, she splashed cold water on her face and ran a brush through her hair. Then she went back into the living room and curled up in the chair again, tucking an afghan about her legs. She sat there—alone and more lonely than she had ever been in her life.

When the knock came at the kitchen door, Chelsie first thought she was imagining things. Then it came again, louder and stronger this time. She quickly padded across the room and into the kitchen beyond. Pressing her face against the cold wood frame, she hesitated a moment.

"W-Who is it?" she finally whispered, scarcely loud enough to be heard on the other side.

"Drew."

Joy, sadness, regret, even a spark of fear ran through her at the sound of his voice.

"Chelsie—it's Drew. Let me in."

She slipped off the chain lock and turned the knob. There he stood. He made an imposing figure, standing tall in the pale beam of light cast by the open doorway. He was still wearing the same three-piece suit she had seen him in earlier that day. He looked tired and there were lines around his eyes and at the corners of his mouth that she had not noticed before. Perhaps they had not been there before, she thought, suddenly guilt-stricken.

"H-Hello," she murmured, almost to herself.

"Hello?" The word was repeated with ill-concealed sarcasm. Drew ran a hand through his hair in a gesture of suppressed anger and frustration. "God—you look awful," he said, without meaning to speak aloud.

"If you think this is bad, you should have seen me a

half hour ago," Chelsie said, with a self-deprecating laugh.

"Well—are we going to have this out on your doorstep or do you intend to invite me in?" he muttered impatiently.

"Please—come in," she motioned, knowing he would whether he was invited or not.

Drew stalked past her and then stopped in the middle of the kitchen and looked back at her. Chelsie closed the door and with a gesture of weariness and defeat indicated that he should precede her into the other room. They stood there facing each other for a moment before either of them spoke.

"All right—what the hell is going on?" The words exploded from him as he threw himself into the chair opposite the one she'd been sitting in.

Chelsie felt half dead. She knew she wasn't up to this—not tonight. She wanted to choose her own time and place to confront him, and it wasn't here in the intimacy of her apartment. And it wasn't now.

"Couldn't this wait until tomorrow, Drew?" she asked, eyeing him warily.

"No—it can not wait until tomorrow!" He threw the words back in her face. For the first time he seemed to be on the verge of losing his composure. "Why did you walk out on me?" he asked, coming straight to the point.

Chelsie faltered for a second, suddenly conscious of the rather ridiculous flannel nightgown that covered her from her neck to her ankles. "I-I explained in my note. . . ."

"You explained nothing!" Drew interrupted, in a voice rigid with anger. He took a slip of paper from his coat pocket and held it out to her. She recognized it immediately as the note she had left for him that afternoon. "What the hell is 'we have no future together' supposed to mean?"

Chelsie took the note, scanned the words written in her own hand, and gave it back to him. "It means exactly what it says—we have no future together," she reiterated flatly. "I think we should end our affair now before we get any more involved."

"I've got news for you, sweetheart," Drew growled in a bitingly sarcastic voice. "It's too late. We're already involved—right up to our necks!"

Chelsie heaved a great sigh and reseated herself. She had the feeling it was going to be a long night before all was said and done. She studied her hands for a moment, palms up. Her voice was soft and cold when she spoke next.

"This isn't easy for me, Drew," she began slowly.

"And it isn't going to get any easier," he interposed brusquely.

"It just wouldn't work out between us. You must see that, too," she implored of him. "I want to end it before someone gets hurt."

Drew's expression was icy. "Is that what this is really all about, Chelsie? Are you afraid of getting hurt?"

"Yes," she said, breathing the word like a curse. "And I know the time would come when I would hurt you, too."

"Well, you're right about that, babe. You're tearing my guts apart right now." Drew's voice broke for a second. "Dammit, Chelsie, I don't understand!" The note he had been holding in his hand was now crumpled in an angry fist. "I thought you were in love with me?" He made it a question.

"I—I am—" she replied, her voice shaking with

emotion. She couldn't bring herself to lie to him about that. It might be the quickest solution to the problem, to tell him that she didn't love him and wanted out, but dear God—she just couldn't say the words!

He looked at her long and hard. "If I love you and you love me, then what in the hell is the problem?"

Chelsie allowed her eyes to go wide in surprise. "You—you never said that before—about loving me." It was almost an accusation.

Drew took a deep breath, unconsciously shrugging his shoulders. "I guess I thought you knew by the way I made love to you."

"A woman wants to hear the words, Drew." She made that admission cautiously.

"I love you, Chelsie," he said in a quiet and determined voice. His gaze brushed her face like a touch of need.

Two tears welled from her eyes and ran down her cheeks. "It doesn't change anything, you know. It just makes it that much harder for both of us."

"Why?" He jumped to his feet. "Why does it make it that much harder?"

"Because loving isn't enough sometimes." Chelsie closed her eyes for some seconds. "We're too different, Drew."

"You're right—we are different," he said, in a low, mocking tone. "I'm a man and you're a woman. That's the only difference we have to contend with."

"If only it were that simple. . . ." she murmured wistfully and a little sadly.

"It *is* that simple," Drew said matter-of-factly. "We can make it, babe. I know we can."

Chelsie shook her head all the while he was speaking. "The only thing we would succeed in doing is making each other miserable. We'd end up hating each other, Drew. Don't you see—we're two different kinds of people? I can't be the woman you want and you can't be the man I need."

His lips went white. "Dammit, Chelsie, you *are* the woman I want!"

"Yes, in bed—but there's more to life than making love," she said, her voice sharp with tension. "I can't change who or what I am, not even for you. I don't belong in your world and I never will."

"We never should have gone to Albany," muttered Drew, as if he'd like to kick himself. "It was something that happened this weekend, wasn't it? What was it, Chelsie?"

"It wasn't any *one* thing," she replied, with a trace of impatience.

"It was the Allens' party." He made it a statement of fact. "I had a feeling you didn't care much for that kind of affair."

"Oh—you don't know the half of it!" she laughed raggedly, suddenly angry herself. It was all going to come out now, every gory detail. "Not only was I left on my own with a roomful of strangers for most of the evening, not only did I spend a 'fascinating' half hour talking to a woman who had never even heard of Chaucer—but the real icing on the cake came when your old girlfriend, the worse for wear, accosted me in front of everyone. You're right about one thing, Drew. I *don't* care much for that kind of affair!"

He was following her words with the closest attention. "What old girlfriend?" he asked, a puzzled expression on his face.

She made a disparaging sound. "Monica Wells."

"For God's sake, honey, Monica Wells isn't an old

girlfriend of mine. We only went out together two or three times and that was over a year ago. The woman is a damned lush—everybody knows that."

"*I* didn't! Not until I had the distinct pleasure of meeting Miss Wells," she said, her voice filled with contempt.

"I'll see to it that she extends a public apology to you," he stated, his mouth held in a thin line.

"That's not the point." Chelsie threw her hands up in frustration. "Oh, Drew—don't you see? A man in your position has to attend all kinds of social functions like the one at the Allens'. I'm no good at that kind of thing. I detest big parties!"

"You want to call it off between us because you dislike big parties?" His expression was one of incredulity.

"Don't be absurd," she countered indignantly. "It's not the parties, it's what they represent. It's your whole life style I can't handle—your money and your fancy cars and that apartment. . . ."

Drew stopped pacing the floor in front of her long enough to give Chelsie a withering glance. "I'm not going to apologize for having money."

"A great deal of money," she said in a dry voice.

"All right—a great deal of money."

"I don't want you to apologize. I'm just trying to make you understand we're not the same kind of people."

"Why? Because I drive a Mercedes while you have an AMC Eagle? Now who's being absurd?" he snapped.

"I don't know how to make you understand," Chelsie murmured, with more than a suspicion of tears in her voice. "If you were really *Professor* Andrew

Bradford we might have a chance, but as it is. . . ."
She opened her arms wide and let them fall in a
gesture of futility.

Drew stopped dead in his tracks. "Are you trying to
tell me that if I give up Bradford Electronics I can have
you in exchange?" There was something in his voice
that Chelsie didn't like.

"No—" she swallowed with difficulty, "I'm not. I
would never want any man to give up his life for me.
And Bradford Electronics is your life, Drew." She
looked up at him with a clear, purposeful blue gaze.
"You need that company as much as it needs you. You
can't turn your back and just walk away. It's a matter
of responsibility over personal desire."

He caught hold of her unceremoniously by the
shoulders. "So where does that leave us, babe? You
and me? A man and a woman who love each other,
who want each other. What about us?" His voice held
an unsteady note.

It was almost Chelsie's undoing. "We—we each go
our separate ways. We have no other choice," she
mumbled into the collar of her nightgown.

Drew put a hand under her chin and forced her to
look at him. "You can sit there and in one breath tell
me that you love me and in the next that we have to
go our separate ways. What runs through your veins,
Dr. McBride? Ice water?" he said, in a voice laced
heavily with bitterness.

Chelsie flinched visibly. "I thought you were many
things, Drew Bradford, but not cruel—never that," she
choked, genuinely wounded by his scathing remark.

"Damn, honey, I'm fighting for my life!" He
dropped his hands from her shoulders and straightened up. He stepped away from her and stood gazing

out the living room window for some minutes before he spoke again. "Do you know what I was going to do after the party tonight?" he asked, without turning around.

"No—" Chelsie whispered, holding her breath.

"I was going to ask you to marry me," Drew said, in a very hard, dry voice. "I've never asked that of any woman."

Oh, dear God! Chelsie silently agonized. Squeezing her eyes tightly shut, she bit down on the inside of her lip until she drew blood. It was the only way she could keep herself from crying out. She couldn't seem to breathe. It was as if she was suffocating.

"While I hardly expected brass bands to play, I thought you might have something to say to that," he went on, swinging back around to face her.

Chelsie's eyes fluttered open as she made herself look Drew straight in the face. "I—I wish I could marry you," she said in an odd little voice that didn't sound like her at all.

Drew was as tense and watchful as a big jungle cat crouched in tall grass waiting for its prey. "You can—just say the word."

"I can't!" she groaned.

"You mean, you won't," Drew stated, without a shred of mercy.

"Damn you, Drew Bradford!" Chelsie cried out, tears clouding her vision. "Why do I have to be the villain of the piece? Why do I have to be the one to say no? You're tearing me apart. Don't you see that? It's like dangling a feast in front of a starving man, but not letting him have even one bite. I love you. I want to be your wife. But if we did get married the way things are now, we wouldn't make it to the first anniversary. I guarantee it. Only a fool believes that love is the only thing a man and woman need to make a relationship work. You're either a fool, which I seriously doubt, or you are deliberately closing your eyes to reality. We are supposed to be two mature adults. When are you going to start acting like one?" It was Chelsie's turn to show no mercy.

His lips tightened in an angry line. His gray eyes blazed with fury. "I'm a fool because I believe we can make it and you don't? Because I think the way we feel about each other is the most important thing?" He let each word fall as if it were a dagger. "Well, I told you after we made love the first time that our relationship would be either a one-night stand or a whole lot more. I warned you then that if we made love again I would never be able to let you go. Well—we made love again this morning, babe, and now I have no intention of letting you walk out of my life. You're mine, Chelsie. You're going to stay mine. I want you!"

"We can't always have what we want," she said in a small, but firm voice.

Driven by a force stronger than himself, Drew grasped her by the shoulders and lifted her right out of the chair and into his arms.

"Don't tell me that you can give this up so easily," he growled against her mouth, as he laid claim to that which he said was his.

He wrapped his arms around her like a velvet vise; his lips overwhelmed hers as he pressed her against his hungry body. And Chelsie found herself responding with a hunger as great as his own. Dear God—to show her what heaven could be just before snapping it out of her reach!

"Now look at me and tell me you can't marry me,"

he said with a self-satisfied expression on his face, as he drew away from her.

Chelsie pulled herself together with a visible effort. "I can not marry you," she replied slowly, her words widely spaced. He started to take her in his arms again. "No—don't!" Chelsie cried out. "If you love me then don't make this any harder for me than it already is. Please, Drew." She begged him with her heart in her eyes.

Something seemed to go out of him then. Some vitality in him flickered and died. "How can I just walk away from you?" he demanded lifelessly.

She knew he was angry and he was hurting—but it was nothing compared to the hurt she would cause him if she gave in now. She must be strong for both their sakes.

"You have to walk out that door tonight and not come back. It's the only way," Chelsie said quietly, undoing her hand from his.

He studied her for a moment or two. "Is that your final word?"

"That is my final word," she said in a low voice, but her words carried the full weight of her determination behind them. She knew he wouldn't ask again. After all, he was a man who had his pride, too.

Drew abruptly turned and walked away from her. He paused with his hand on the kitchen door and looked back at Chelsie for a moment.

"I hope you know you have just condemned me to a living hell, babe."

He smashed his fist into the door frame and then with a lift of his shoulders, Drew Bradford opened the door and walked out of her apartment and out of her life.

Chelsie stood there, staring at the door, wanting to call out Drew's name—wanting to call him back into her arms. But in the end, she let him go without a word.

Chelsie didn't sleep at all that night or the next, and even when she finally could she spent most of the night tossing and turning. She began to wear tinted glasses to obscure the fact that she had spent too many sleepless nights of late. She lost weight, as well, and her once curvaceous figure now bordered on the slender.

She thought about calling Drew a dozen times or more, even going so far as to dial his telephone number one night when she didn't think she could go another moment without hearing his voice. There had been no answer, and when she recovered her senses the next day she was almost relieved that he had not been at home. It would have been awkward for both of them—she realized that in the clear light of day. For what could she have said to him that would not have been hurtful or even embarrassing for her?

Drew had made no effort to see her again after the scene in her apartment that night. What had she expected? That was the question Chelsie asked herself a hundred times. She had told him in no uncertain terms that she did not want to see him again, that they had no future together. And Drew Bradford was definitely not the kind of man to chase after a woman who had told him that. He was a man with immense pride, and no doubt there were plenty of women ready to console him if he did indeed require any consoling.

In the weeks that followed, Chelsie discovered much to her surprise that two people could avoid each other rather effectively on the relatively small campus of the state university. She did catch a glimpse of Drew in the distance every now and then and there were several times when they unavoidably passed each other in the halls. He merely inclined his head and muttered, "Dr. McBride," before passing on by her.

Those were the times when Chelsie wondered if she had not been the bigger fool of the two of them. There was the man she loved and who supposedly loved her, and she had thrown their future away simply because she believed they would make each other unhappy one day. Those were the times when she wished she had just lived for the moment and not worried about the day of reckoning. Perhaps it was wiser to live only for the present and let the future take care of itself. But that wasn't the way she was made, and it was too late to try to change nearly twenty-nine years of becoming what she was.

No one knew that the young English professor was walking around with a heart that had turned into a cold hard stone. Even Lynn Marshall had accepted without question the brief explanation Chelsie gave her—that she and Drew had mutually agreed to stop seeing each other when they found they had so little in common. No one knew that she and Drew had been lovers, she was certain of that—except the two of them, of course.

More than once, Chelsie had nearly approached Dr. Nelson about terminating her sabbatical early. Each time a half-dozen arguments came to mind that stopped her from seeking him out to that purpose.

She had no apartment to return to at Bryn Mawr and no job until after the first of the year. She could not afford to forfeit her salary at the state university even if she did have a place to go. Not only that, her reputation was at stake, as well.

Dr. Chelsie McBride had never been a quitter, and to run away under circumstances that would have been impossible to explain was not her style. She knew that even if she did manage to run away from Oneonta, she could not run from the pain in her heart every time she thought of Drew and what they might have had together.

After the first three weeks, Chelsie had pulled herself together enough to be sure that she could make it to the end of the semester knowing that Drew was often in the same building—knowing that his house was only a few minutes from where she was struggling to read the midterms on Chaucer that her class had taken that day. She forced herself to become absorbed in her work to the exclusion of all else. She had no other choice.

In a strange way, she recognized that it would be difficult for her to leave Oneonta when her time here was up. The chances of seeing Drew again once she left the central New York State community would fall to zero. The occasional glimpses she had of him were both the source of great pain and great joy to her.

Chelsie McBride would never be the same woman again, she knew that now. She had already decided that she would finish out the year at Bryn Mawr and then go on to something else. She had been seriously considering putting her name in with a school over-seas. If she needed a complete change of scenery,

then why not make it as far from this part of the world
as she could? New faces in a new place might be just
what the doctor would order.

The Christmas season was upon her before Chelsie
knew it. She did some shopping for her family in
Breese's, the biggest department store Oneonta had
to offer. It brought back memories of other Christ-
mases long past when she had shopped there as a girl.
They would all be gathering at her brother Stephen's
house this year in Pittsburgh. For the first time in her
life, Chelsie wasn't sure she could face her family at
what was supposed to be the most joyous season of
the year. This would have been her first Christmas
with Drew—and the thought sent her dashing from
more than one store before the tears that threatened
to fall could materialize.

What hurt most were the love songs written about
the season. "Chestnuts Roasting on an Open Fire"
and "I'll Be Home for Christmas" gave her the most
difficult moments of all. She knew that they were
songs that she and Drew would never share now.
They had had so little time together when all was said
and done. A few short weeks of happiness that would
have to last her a lifetime. It was more than she could
bear to think about at times.

And then the day came when final exams were over
and the grades were posted. There was nothing to
prevent her from leaving now. It was time to go back
to her apartment and load her car and the familiar
U-haul and be on her way. She had the drive to Bryn
Mawr tomorrow to unload her things and then the
very next day she was scheduled to get into her Eagle
again and make the trip to Pittsburgh.

Chelsie gathered up her belongings from the cubicle that had been her office for the past four months and walked out the door for the last time. There was no sense in putting it off any longer. She would be up late finishing her packing as it was. Resolutely, she walked down the empty hall, her briefcase in hand, and went out into the wintry afternoon air.

9

~~~~~~~~~~

Back at her apartment, Chelsie changed into a pair of serviceable jeans and a turtleneck sweater that had seen better days. Then without further delay she pushed up her sleeves and got to work. She had her books and papers and a few articles of clothing left to pack before she tackled the assorted items in the kitchen that had accumulated during the semester.

She decided to pack her stereo last, although most of her records were already in a box. She wandered over to the half-dozen or so records she had left out and chose the *Peer Gynt Suite* by Grieg to help make the time packing less laborious. It seemed like a good idea until the strains of "Solvejg's Song"—the soulful lament of lost love—came wafting across the room. The lilting but depressing music drove her to remove the record and replace it with an upbeat recording of classical jazz.

There—that was better! thought Chelsie, as she

tackled the last box of books and set them in the middle of the floor until Mrs. Freeman's nephew could come by later and help her take the heaviest things down to her car. The stereo would have to wait until morning so that it would not sit out in the zero degree temperatures overnight.

For the next two hours, she worked with unflagging energy until a rumbling in her stomach reminded her that the dinner hour had passed. She stopped long enough to fix herself a bowl of clam chowder— canned, not homemade.

Chelsie was rinsing her dishes in the sink when a knock sounded at the inside door of her apartment. For just a moment, her heart seemed to stop beating, but it resumed its rhythmic force when she saw Lynn Marshall standing there in the hallway.

"Hi, Lynn." She greeted her friend with genuine cheerfulness. "You must have read my mind. I was going to stop by your place in about five minutes."

"I wanted to come by to say happy holidays and bon voyage before you head out in the morning. This is for you," Lynn murmured, handing Chelsie a small package she had in her hands. "Merry Christmas!"

"Oh, Lynn. . . ." Tears came to Chelsie's eyes. "Can you come in for a minute?" she sniffed. "I have something for you, too. Find a place to sit, if you can," she invited with a half laugh. "I'm in a terrible mess again, as you can see." Chelsie took a gift-wrapped box safely set to one side and offered it to the other woman. "Merry Christmas to you, too, Lynn."

"Are we going to wait until the twenty-fifth?" grinned Lynn, in an attempt to lighten their mood.

"You've got to be kidding!" exclaimed Chelsie, looking down at the half-unwrapped gift on her lap.

She was the first to have hers out of its box. It was a bottle of her favorite perfume. "How thoughtful, Lynn. I didn't realize you'd noticed," she said in a soft voice.

"Oh, Chelsie—it's lovely!" exclaimed the brunette, as she removed the delicate music box from its wrappings. She opened the lid with the rose on the top and the tinkling melody of "La Vie en Rose" filled the room. "Thank you," Lynn smiled, gently closing the lid.

"So—what are your plans for the holidays?" Chelsie asked, with a watery smile.

"I'm going home with Frank tonight to meet his parents," Lynn confessed with a sly grin. "Then we'll both be coming back here on Christmas Day to have dinner with my family."

Chelsie raised one brow in simulated surprise. "Lynn Marshall, are you trying to tell me something?"

"I told Frank he would have his answer by New Year's, but I think it's going to be yes," Lynn announced with thoughtful restraint. "I'm twenty-seven years old, Chelsie, and I figure if I have to take the chance it might as well be with Frank. Besides—I happen to love the man."

"I won't say a word until it's official, but congratulations!" Chelsie said, giving Lynn a big hug.

"What about you?" asked the brunette. "What are your plans for Christmas?"

"My whole family will be at my brother's for the big celebration," Chelsie replied, with more enthusiasm than she actually felt. "I'll be driving to Pittsburgh the day after tomorrow."

"Do you plan to see Drew Bradford before you leave?" Lynn asked in all innocence.

"No, I'm not planning to see him again," Chelsie said with an unhappy attempt at lightness.

Apparently the other woman couldn't leave the subject of Andrew Bradford alone. "You know—for a while there at the beginning of the semester, I thought you two might have something going."

"No—we didn't have anything going for us," Chelsie stated, with a cold finality that convinced even Lynn Marshall to drop the subject once and for all.

"I guess I'd better be going," the brunette said, getting to her feet. "I still have to decide what dress to wear to meet Frank's mother and father. I do want to make a good first impression."

"I'm sure they'll love you," Chelsie murmured encouragingly.

"I'm going to miss you, you know that," Lynn said, as she paused at the apartment door. "It's been fun, Chelsie."

"Yes, it has. I'll try to write—honestly, I will," she vowed, "but letter writing has never been one of my strong points."

"And you an English professor," teased Lynn. "Take care, Chel!"

"Merry Christmas, Lynn!" Chelsie called after her friend as she went down the hall and into her own apartment.

Chelsie admitted to a few minutes of self-pity after Lynn's departure, but self-pity took time and energy she simply did not have to waste on such an unproductive pastime. She still had hours of packing ahead of her.

It was nearly ten o'clock that night before Chelsie took a much needed and much deserved break, but she could do so with a real feeling of accomplishment. She had everything done, down to laying out her slacks and sweater for the drive tomorrow and the box for packing the coffeepot that still stood on the kitchen counter.

But it wasn't coffee she was having for her break. It was wine. She had nearly half a bottle left in the refrigerator and she wasn't about to pour it down the drain! Instead, she poured it into her coffee cup and lit a cigarette. Chelsie didn't think she was ever going to make a smoker. She was up to a pack of cigarettes a week now and that was only through a great deal of effort.

She had just inhaled the first puff when a second knock came at her apartment door. She'd thought she had heard Lynn leave earlier in the evening, but perhaps it was Esther Freeman come to say her farewells. Past caring at this point, Chelsie went to answer the door with the cigarette in one hand and the cup of wine in the other. She called out a greeting to the impatient visitor and did some quick juggling with the wine and cigarette, managing to open the door on the second knock.

"Hello, Chelsie," came the painfully familiar accents of Drew Bradford's resonant baritone. She promptly proceeded to choke on her cigarette. Evidently Drew felt compelled to step forward and give her a resounding slap on the back, for that is exactly what he did. "Nasty habit—smoking," he said in a lazy drawl.

"It's an infrequent habit, as habits go," she mumbled, not very subtly masking her annoyance.

Drew went on smoothly, his eyes on her. "May I come in?"

"You are in," Chelsie stated cryptically.

"I guess I am," he admitted with what sounded suspiciously like a chuckle. Drew paused and then said in a different voice, "I see you're packing."

"Yes—I drive back to Bryn Mawr in the morning," she said, in a conversational tone. Chelsie felt pleased with the way she had tossed that off so nonchalantly. "My time here at Oneonta is up, you know."

A scowl creased his forehead. "Yes, I'm aware of that. It's one of the reasons I stopped by tonight. I just didn't think you would be leaving so soon."

"I have no reason not to leave," she said with a touch of reproach.

"Could I have some of that coffee?" Drew inquired, gesturing toward her cup.

"It's not coffee—it's wine—but you're welcome to join me if you wish," she said, meeting his inquiring gaze.

"Thanks, I will then," he replied, moving a box of books off one of her chairs as if it weighed nothing at all. He hurled himself into the chair and took out a pack of cigarettes.

"You'll have to excuse the cup. All my glasses are packed," Chelsie explained, handing him a cup of wine indentical to her own. "I thought you said smoking was a nasty habit," she remarked, repeating his earlier sentiments.

"It is," Drew said, lighting the cigarette anyway. "You look thinner," he commented, running his eyes down her body.

"I went on a diet," she offered, with a descriptive wrinkling of her nose.

"You didn't need to lose any weight," he murmured

tactfully. "If I remember correctly you had a perfect figure the way you were," he added.

"Then I guess it's a matter of personal preference," she responded, choosing to ignore the innuendo in his comment.

"How have you been, Chelsie?" Drew finally asked, as if he wasn't sure what to say next.

"Fine," she replied blithely. "And yourself?" she inquired with a nod of her head.

Drew set his wine on the table at his elbow and thrust out his hands. He studied the palms for some moments before he replied. "I've been busy."

"Doing anything in particular?" Chelsie asked in a voice mellowed by her second cup of wine.

Drew frowned slightly as he folded his arms across his chest. He ventured to lift his head and ran his eyes over her, watching for any signs of reaction. "I have been involved in moving the research and development department of Bradford Electronics from Albany to Oneonta."

"How nice—" Chelsie said inanely, failing to see any special significance in his announcement.

"I've reached a decision about my future with Bradford Electronics," he stated, in a louder voice.

"That's right—you had to give the Board of Directors your answer by Christmas," she murmured. "Well, I'm sure you made the right decision, Drew."

"Dammit, Chelsie, don't you even care to hear what I've decided to do?" His voice rose, heavy with anger.

Chelsie was utterly taken aback. Her forehead creased a moment perplexedly. "Of course, I want to hear your decision. I—I just thought you had undoubtedly decided to give up your teaching position and return to Albany at the end of the year."

"Well, you thought wrong!" Drew said with some heat. "I'm not going back to Albany."

"You're not going back to Albany?" she repeated unsteadily, her heart beginning to pick up speed.

"No, I'm not," Drew said in a quiet and determined voice. "And do you know why?"

Chelsie found his inquiry unexpectedly difficult to answer. "No—I don't know why."

Drew gave her a quick questioning look. "I'm not going back to Albany because I have turned down the presidency of Bradford Electronics. I am going to head up the research and development division of the company here."

"Are you sure that's what you want to do?" she asked, after the briefest of pauses. "I mean it will be so different from being the head of the corporation," she sighed, unconsciously straightening her shoulders.

"That's what I'm counting on," he replied, in his softest tone. "Chelsie—I—I want to ask you something."

Something in his tone made her glance up at him, but his expression told her nothing. "Yes?" she asked, her brows drawing together in a thoughtful frown.

"May I have a refill on the wine?" he said in a brisk tone.

"Of course," she answered, getting to her feet. She walked over to Drew and reached for the cup on the table beside him.

He was very quiet. Then he caught his breath; it sounded like a groan. "I don't really want any more wine," he confessed, grasping her wrist in his hand.

"Then what do you want?" Chelsie said, looking down at him, uncomprehending.

"This!" Drew muttered, as he gave her wrist a jerk, pulling her down onto his lap. "I want this!"

His mouth captured hers in an explosion of desire and need as all the pent-up emotions of the past months sprang to the surface. This was no gentle, exploratory kiss—but the fierce, driving hunger of a man who had been to hell and back for this moment. And suddenly, Chelsie knew that this was all that mattered—to be in Drew's arms. Given a second chance, she would do anything to make this moment last.

He kissed her again and again and she found herself responding instinctively, until the first outburst of rediscovery was satisfied and Drew could treat her with the tenderness she desired. He held her within his embrace then, as his lips buried themselves in the soft folds of her hair.

"Oh, babe—I've needed to do this for so damned long!" he muttered in a husky voice, inhaling the very scent of her. "I've wanted to come to you so many times . . . you have no idea how many. God, I've missed this!" he said, putting a hand on her breast.

Something inside Chelsie grew cold at his touch. He had said he missed *this,* not that he had missed *her,* and she knew full well what Drew meant by *this.* She firmly removed his hand and started to get up from his lap, her face red with indignation.

"What's the matter, honey?" he asked, genuinely puzzled by her sudden coolness toward him.

"Let go of me, Drew," she gritted through her teeth.

"What the hell?" he sputtered, refusing to do as she bid. "A minute ago you were all soft and warm and willing," he said, with summary bluntness.

"That was a minute ago," she replied, head cocked. "Now I want you to let me go."

"All right, I'll let you go—but only if you tell me what's the matter."

"Let me go first," Chelsie bargained, having no intention of explaining herself when he did.

"Tell me first!" Drew countered, holding the upper hand.

She gave it about thirty seconds of thought before answering. "I don't care to be regarded as a sex object by any man."

"Sex object?" He burst out laughing, but broke off at the sight of Chelsie's perfectly serious face. "You can't believe that sex is all I came here for tonight," he roared, angry himself now.

Chelsie flung up her defiant chin and fixed Drew with large, reproachful blue eyes. "What else am I to think?"

"You could at least give me the benefit of the doubt," he replied, with a sense of injury. "Why do you think I was going on and on about my decision to refuse the presidency of Bradford Electronics?" She shook her head. "I was trying to tell you that I have changed my life style—the life style you so violently opposed the last time we were together."

"I—I don't understand." Chelsie's voice held an unsteady note.

"Apparently not," Drew muttered, his tone dry and brusque. "We seem to have our share of communication problems."

Chelsie quit her struggles and gave Drew a long, measuring look. "Exactly why did you come here tonight?" she asked, biting her lip.

His eyes, cool rather than hostile, touched hers briefly. "I came here tonight to ask you to come back to me."

Chelsie's heart slammed against her chest. "Come back to you?"

"Yes, I thought you might change your mind about marrying me if you knew that things were different," he said, with a touch of impatience.

"And are things really different now, Drew? Are you happy with the decision you made about the company?" she asked, as if her entire future depended on his answer.

"At first, I wasn't sure, to be honest with you," Drew said thoughtfully. "But as the negotiations progressed to move the research and development department I found I was happier than I'd been in years. I know now I made the right decision."

"Then—yes, I will," Chelsie said, still shaking with reaction.

"Yes, you will what?" Drew asked in his softest tone.

"Yes, I will marry you, Andrew Bradford—if the offer is still open," she replied, her heart drumming violently.

He gave her that appraising, narrow stare again. "The offer is still open." Then he lost his aloofness as his mouth found hers in a kiss that held passion at bay while he told her of his gratitude. "You don't know how many times I have wanted to hear you say that, Chelsie."

"I know how many times I've wanted to say it," she murmured, covering his face with light little butterfly kisses.

Drew finally pulled back and settled her in his arms. "We have to finish talking."

"Now?" Chelsie asked, as if he were crazy. Who wanted to talk anymore at a time like this?

"Yes, *now*, and behave yourself," he said in a firm voice, folding her hands together in her lap. "And keep them there," Drew scolded. "At least for now."

Chelsie boldly stuck her tongue out at him. "Spoilsport!"

"Oh, you'll get plenty of 'sport' later, honey, if that's what you want," he said, the message in his eyes clearly readable.

"Promises—promises—" she sighed, finally content to curl up in his arms and allow him the chance to say whatever it was he was all fired up to say.

"I want you to believe that we're going to make it, Chelsie. I know we will. I can't promise you I'll be home every night on time for dinner, but I won't be working any weekends from here on out."

"And big parties?" she teased, with a lift of one brow.

"No more than two or three a year and you'll be amply rewarded for putting up with that many," he muttered, dropping a kiss on her mouth.

"And old girlfriends?" she murmured between kisses.

"What old girlfriends?" Drew echoed. "I have only one girl from now on."

"Then I accept the terms of your agreement as you have just outlined them, Mr. Andrew Bradford. Can we stop talking now?" Chelsie pleaded, wrapping her arms around his neck and pressing herself into his lean muscular body.

"I think our communication problems are over, sweetheart," he said with relish, as he gave up any hope or desire of talking further.

Their mouths came together then in a sweet search that told them they would have the rest of their lives to make up for the past months of deprivation. With an arrowed tongue, Drew parted her lips and drank deeply of her, sending odd little quakes down Chelsie's body. She pressed even closer to him and flicked her tongue along his bottom lip in a tickling, teasing manner that drove him to groan her name aloud.

His hands were not inactive for long as he sought out the tempting curves of her body. They caressed her from shoulder to thigh as though he had to be sure she was real and not some figment of his imagination. He clasped her waist between his palms and found the way beneath the confining turtleneck she wore.

"Oh, babe, did you wear this damn sweater on purpose?" Drew groaned, frustrated by its limiting features.

"No more than you did," Chelsie breathed, her own hands snaking under the pullover he wore.

Impatient, and yet gentle, he pulled the turtleneck over her head and let it drop to the floor beside them. Chelsie sat there on his knees, the lacy bra her only covering. She shivered for a moment at the impact of the night air on her bare skin.

"I'm cold," she murmured, wrapping her arms around herself.

"You won't be cold for long," he promised in a husky voice as he slipped the pullover off his body and drew her against the warmth of his flesh.

With fingers that trembled ever so slightly, Drew undid the single hook between her breasts and then her lacy bra joined their sweaters on the floor. Chelsie went to him then, pressing herself against his chest, the fine hair tickling her skin.

He drew her head down to his shoulder as one hand captured its prize and molded it to his liking. He caressed and fingered the pliant nipple until it rose up into an erect bud that pleaded for his touch. Then he bent his head and grasped the nipple in his mouth. The erotic manipulation sent a moan to Chelsie's lips as she caught the hair at his nape in her fingers.

And when Drew sought to slip his hand beneath the waistband of her slacks, another moan issued forth from Chelsie, letting him know once again that his touch set her ablaze. He went further, caressing the sensitive spot between her thighs until she was writhing with pleasure and whimpering his name over and over. Chelsie ran her hand down the male thigh until Drew, too, reacted with a passionate mumbling of his own need.

"Oh, honey—I'm too old to make love in a chair," he finally said, throwing his head back in exasperation.

"I have a better idea," Chelsie offered, her voice made husky by her aroused emotions.

She slipped off his lap and stood in front of him for a moment, looking intently into his eyes. Then she held out her hand to him. He placed his hand in hers and got to his feet.

"Chelsie?"

"Come with me, Andrew Bradford. There's a lesson or two you need to be taught," she murmured, a seductive smile on her lips.

"I've always wanted to be the teacher's pet," he replied eagerly, following her lead as she walked into the next room.

They slowly completed the job of undressing each other and stretched out on the bed, going into one another's arms as though the journey had been a long one indeed. They rediscovered all the little pleasures they had once given each other and yet every pleasure seemed new somehow in the light of their love. Drew stroked her body until Chelsie was sure she would curl up and cease to breathe right there and then.

Her hands began to move with a mind of their own, needing to touch him, to coax him to the same feverish pitch of excitement that gripped her. She found herself aroused by the feel of him as much as he was by her.

"I like your method of teaching, Dr. McBride," Drew whispered against her mouth, as he sought to draw the very breath from her lungs.

"Demonstration has always been an effective teaching tool," she murmured, running her hand down the length of male leg within her reach.

Then he paved the way for their mutual pleasure, seeking the soft, warm inner recesses of her body with his fingers, bringing her to the brink of explosive desire again and again until Chelsie was twisting and turning beneath his touch. Unable to wait any longer for his passionate possession, she reached for him and drew him to her.

"I love you, Drew!" she vowed, with all the emotion that was within her heart.

"And I love you, babe! You're mine now and

forever!" He proved the truth of his claim by thrusting himself into her in the ultimate act that was possession above all others.

And when the explosion came—it came for them as one. They were hurled out into space, their minds and bodies free of all other sensations, until at last they descended together. They held each other then, realizing how close they had come to losing this miracle that happened between them. And it was there in each other's arms that they drifted off to sleep.

When Chelsie awoke she was surprised to find that it was still the middle of the night. She carefully raised her head from Drew's shoulder and looked down at him, expecting to see him asleep. Instead, his eyes were wide open and he was watching her. He gently drew her down beside him, his gaze never leaving her face.

"Happy?" Drew asked, though he knew the answer just from looking at her.

"Happier than I've ever been in my life," she sighed, snuggling up to his welcome warmth.

"I've been thinking," he began, "about when we can get married. I've decided on this weekend."

"You've decided on this weekend!" Chelsie echoed. "But I'm supposed to drive to Pennsylvania tomorrow . . . this morning, that is, and then on to Pittsburgh the next day. My whole family will be there in a few days for Christmas."

"I'm not going to spend another night without you beside me, babe, and that's final," Drew stated in a voice that would brook no argument. "So—unless you want to shock a whole houseful of relatives by bringing your lover along for the holidays, you'd better marry me first," he warned her with a smile—a smile that had a singularly intoxicating quality about it.

"Well—when you put it that way, how can I refuse?" she replied, biting the corners of her mouth against the grin that threatened to form there.

"And as long as you'll be in Oneonta a few extra days, you can talk to Dr. Nelson about a permanent position on the faculty," Drew added. Apparently, he had been awake for some time plotting out their future.

"What if he doesn't want me?" The thought sent a cold shiver of apprehension down Chelsie's spine.

"He will," Drew responded in a brisk tone. "The man's no fool, sweetheart. He'll jump at the chance to hire you away from Bryn Mawr. You have quite a reputation as a Chaucerian scholar, my love. You'd be a feather in the old boy's cap, for sure."

"Gee, I wish you had some confidence in me, darling," Chelsie said, unable to stop herself from grinning now.

"There's only one decision left to make," Drew stated with a perfectly serious expression. "And that's about our house."

"We have to decide about a house *now* in the middle of the night?" she exclaimed, as if she thought he'd lost his mind.

"What do you think about buying the cabin?" he asked, as if he hadn't heard her remark. "I'm renting with an option to purchase the property."

"I love the cabin," Chelsie said, falling in with his plans.

"Then everything is settled," Drew murmured, rolling over on top of her, his intent clear. A glint of satisfaction mingled with desire in his gray eyes. "I have only one regret, babe."

She gazed up at him as his weight bore her down into the bed. "And what's that?" she inquired softly.

"I don't have anything to give you for Christmas," Drew confessed, as his mouth sought hers.

Chelsie smiled up at him then, one finger tracing a lazy pattern against his lip. "Yes, you do, Drew Bradford. Oh, yes, you do."

Then she proceeded to show him exactly what she had in mind.

Silhouette Desire

Six new titles are published on the first Friday every month. All are available at your local bookshop or newsagent, so make sure of obtaining your copies by taking note of the following dates:

APRIL 1st

MAY 6th

JUNE 3rd

JULY 1st

AUGUST 5th

SEPTEMBER 2nd

Now Available

Come Back, My Love by Pamela Wallace

TV newsperson Toni Lawrence was on the fast
track to fame when photographer Theo Chakiris
swept her off her feet at the Royal Wedding.
Storybook romances belonged to princes and
princesses! She tried to forget, to bury herself in
her work, but passion brought them together to
recapture the glory of ecstasy.

Blanket Of Stars by Lorraine Valley

Greece was the perfect setting for adventure and
romance, and for Gena Fielding it became the
land she would call home. In Alex Andreas' dark
eyes she saw a passion and a glory, a flame to
light the way to sensual pleasures and melt her
resistance beneath the searing Greek sun.

Sweet Bondage by Dorothy Vernon

Maxwell Ross had set into motion a plan to avenge his
younger brother. But he was wreaking revenge on the
wrong woman, as Gemma Coleridge was only too
happy to tell him—at first. But soon, too soon, her
heart overrode her head. She lost her anger in
Maxwell's arms, and dared to dream of a happiness
that would last forever.

Now Available

Dream Come True by Ann Major

Six years after their divorce, Barron Skymaster, superstar, tried to claim Amber again. But how could she face him after denying him knowledge of his own son—a son he had every right to know? Would that knowledge bring them together again or would it tear them apart forever?

Of Passion Born by Suzanne Simms

Professor Chelsie McBride was thoroughly acquainted with her subject—the sometimes humorous, sometimes bawdy Canterbury Tales. A respected professional in her field, she was no stranger to the earthy side of passion. But when it was introduced to her in the person of Drew Bradford, she realized she'd only been studying love by the book.

Second Harvest by Erin Ross

The fields of Kia Ora were all that remained of Alex's turbulent past, and Lindsay was bound to honour her husband's memory by taking an active part in the New Zealand vineyard. But what she began with reluctance soon became a fervent obsession. The exotic splendour of Kia Ora was captivating, and Philip Macek, its hard-driving owner, held her spellbound.

Coming Next Month

Lover In Pursuit by Stephanie James

Reyna McKenzie vowed she'd never again succumb to Trevor Langdon's promise of love. But he'd come to Hawaii determined to reclaim her and under the tropical sun, she soon found herself willing to submit to the love she so desperately wanted.

King of Diamonds by Penny Allison

Carney Gallagher was baseball's golden boy, now in the troubled last season. Flame-haired Jo Ryan, the Atlanta *Star's* rookie woman sports reporter, made her first career hit at his expense. Gallagher vowed to even the score . . . but Jo never imagined that passion would be the weapon of his choice.

Love In The China Sea by Judith Baker

Kai Shanpei, mysterious Eurasian tycoon, was as much a part of Hong Kong as its crescent harbour, teeming streets and the jagged mountains looming above. From the moment she met him Anne Hunter was lost in his spell, plucked from reality and transported into his arms to learn the secrets of love.

Coming Next Month

Bittersweet In Bern by Cheryl Durrant

Gabi Studer couldn't resist Peter Imhof's offer of
work in Switzerland, but she hadn't reckoned on
living in the same magnificent Alpine chalet as
the famed author. Alone together on the
enchanted Swiss mountainside, temptation was
only a kiss away.

Constant Stranger by Linda Sunshine

Murphy Roarke literally knocked Joanna
Davenport off her feet. She'd come to New York
to launch a publishing career, and Roarke had
helped her every step of the way . . . until he
stole her heart, demanding that she choose
between the job of a lifetime and a stormy,
perilous love.

Shared Moments by Mary Lynn Baxter

He was the devil in disguise. Kace McCord, the
silver-haired client Courtney Roberts tried to
keep at arm's length. But he took possession of
her from the first, arousing her feelings and
driving her to heights of rapture.

THE MORE SENSUAL
PROVOCATIVE ROMANCE

95p each

1 ☐ CORPORATE AFFAIR
Stephanie James

2 ☐ LOVE'S SILVER WEB
Nicole Monet

3 ☐ WISE FOLLY
Rita Clay

4 ☐ KISS AND TELL
Suzanne Carey

5 ☐ WHEN LAST WE LOVED
Judith Baker

6 ☐ A FRENCH-MAN'S KISS
Kathryn Mallory

7 ☐ NOT EVEN FOR LOVE
Erin St. Claire

8 ☐ MAKE NO PROMISES
Sherry Dee

9 ☐ MOMENT IN TIME
Suzanne Simms

10 ☐ WHENEVER I LOVE YOU
Alana Smith

11 ☐ VELVET TOUCH
Stephanie James

12 ☐ THE COWBOY AND THE LADY
Diana Palmer

13 ☐ COME BACK MY LOVE
Pamela Wallace

14 ☐ BLANKET OF STARS
Lorraine Valley

15 ☐ SWEET BONDAGE
Dorothy Vernon

16 ☐ DREAM COME TRUE
Ann Major

17 ☐ OF PASSION BORN
Suzanne Simms

18 ☐ SECOND HARVEST
Erin Ross

All these books are available at your local bookshop or newsagent, or can be ordered direct from the publisher. Just tick the titles you want and fill in the form below.

Prices and availability subject to change without notice.

SILHOUETTE BOOKS, P.O. Box 11, Falmouth, Cornwall.

Please send cheque or postal order, and allow the following for postage and packing:

U.K. – 45p for one book, plus 20p for the second book, and 14p for each additional book ordered up to a £1.63 maximum.

B.F.P.O. and EIRE – 45p for the first book, plus 20p for the second book, and 14p per copy for the next 7 books, 8p per book thereafter.

OTHER OVERSEAS CUSTOMERS – 75p for the first book, plus 21p per copy for each additional book.

Name ....

Address ....

....